# Plants vs. Zombies

## LAWN OF DOOM #3

ABDO
Spotlight

DARK
HORSE
BOOKS

PopCap

Written by **PAUL TOBIN**

Art by **RON CHAN**

Colors by **MATT J. RAINWATER**

Letters by **STEVE DUTRO**

Cover by **RON CHAN**

Publisher **MIKE RICHARDSON**
Editor **PHILIP R. SIMON**
Assistant Editor **MEGAN WALKER**
Designer **BRENNAN THOME**
Digital Art Technician **CHRISTINA McKENZIE**

Special thanks to Leigh Beach, Rachel Downing, Alexandria Land, A.J. Rathbun, Kristen Star, and everyone at PopCap Games.

DarkHorse.com
PopCap.com


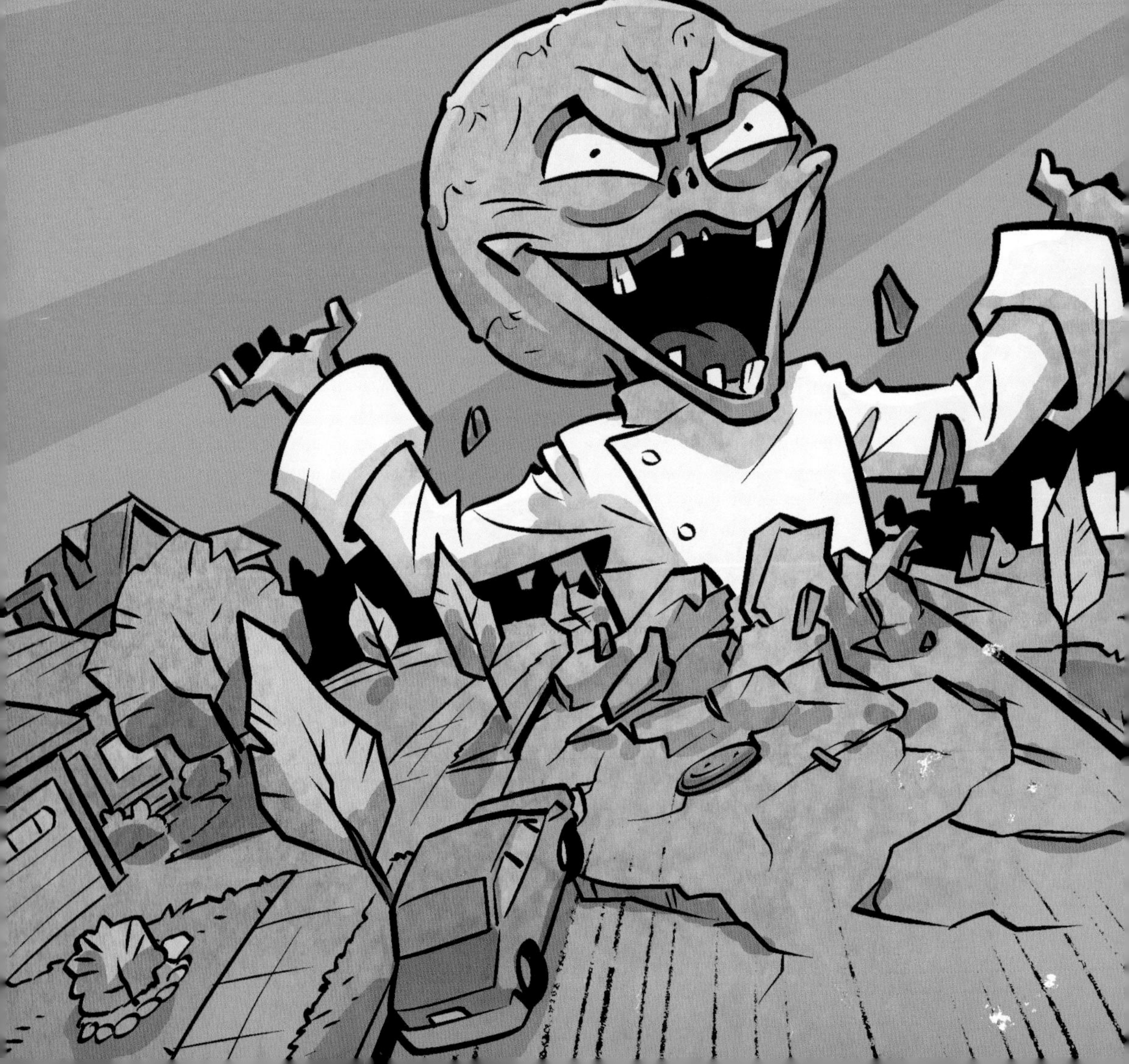

# PLANTS VS. ZOMBIES™

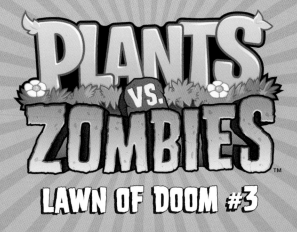

## LAWN OF DOOM #3

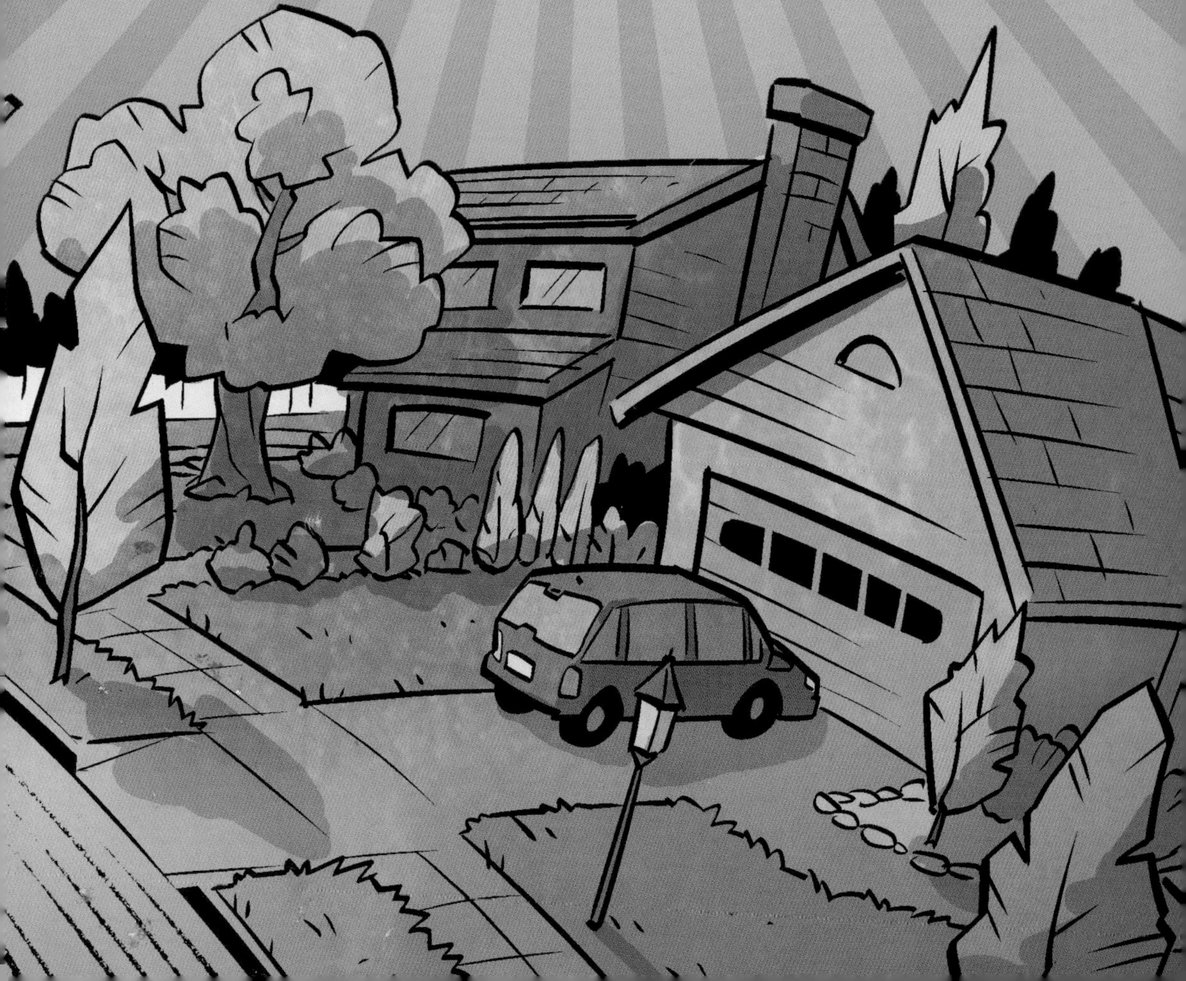

**ABDOBOOKS.COM**

Reinforced library bound edition published in 2020 by Spotlight, a division of ABDO, PO Box 398166, Minneapolis, Minnesota 55439. Spotlight produces high-quality reinforced library bound editions for schools and libraries.
Published by agreement with Dark Horse Comics.

Printed in the United States of America, North Mankato, Minnesota.
042019
092019

THIS BOOK CONTAINS
RECYCLED MATERIALS

*PopCap*

Library of Congress Control Number: 2019938227

Publisher's Cataloging-in-Publication Data

Names: Tobin, Paul, author. | Chan, Ron, illustrator.
Title: Lawn of doom / writer: Paul Tobin; art: Ron Chan.
Description: Minneapolis, Minnesota : Spotlight, 2020 | Series: Plants vs. zombies
Summary: With Zomboss trying to turn Halloween into a Lawn of Doom celebration, Patrice, Nate, Crazy Dave, and the plants fight back in contests of tricks, treats, and costumes.
Identifiers: ISBN 9781532143830 (#1 ; lib. bdg.) | ISBN 9781532143847 (#2 ; lib. bdg.) | ISBN 9781532143854 (#3 ; lib. bdg.)
Subjects: LCSH: Plants vs. zombies (Game)--Juvenile fiction. | Plants--Juvenile fiction. | Zombies--Juvenile fiction. | Halloween--Juvenile fiction. | Graphic novels--Juvenile fiction. | Comic books, strips, etc--Juvenile fiction.
Classification: DDC 741.5--dc23

**Spotlight**

A Division of ABDO
abdobooks.com

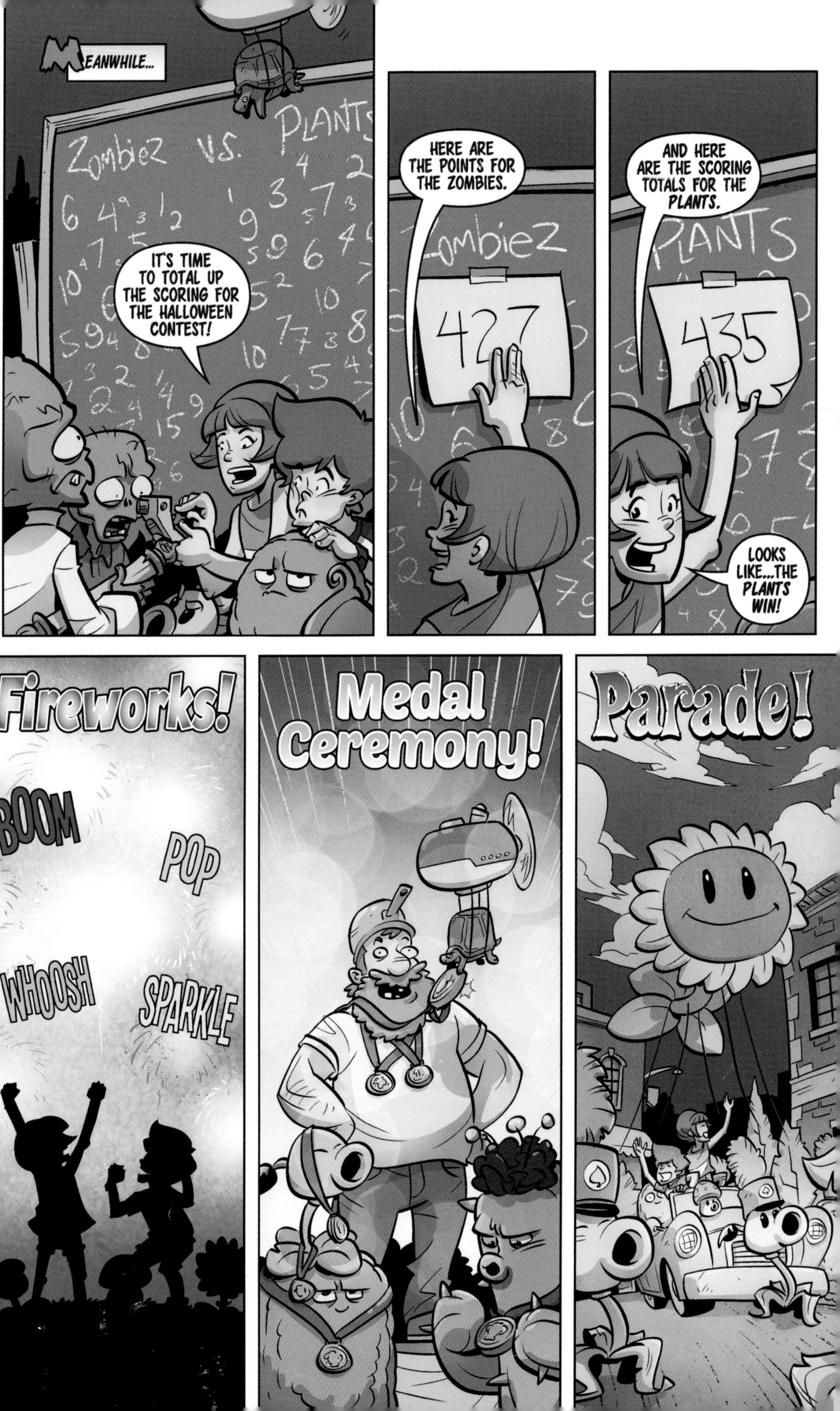
MEANWHILE...
ZOMBIEZ VS. PLANTS
IT'S TIME TO TOTAL UP THE SCORING FOR THE HALLOWEEN CONTEST!
HERE ARE THE POINTS FOR THE ZOMBIES.
ZOMBIEZ
427
AND HERE ARE THE SCORING TOTALS FOR THE PLANTS.
PLANTS
435
LOOKS LIKE...THE PLANTS WIN!
Fireworks!
BOOM
POP
WHOOSH
SPARKLE
Medal Ceremony!
Parade!

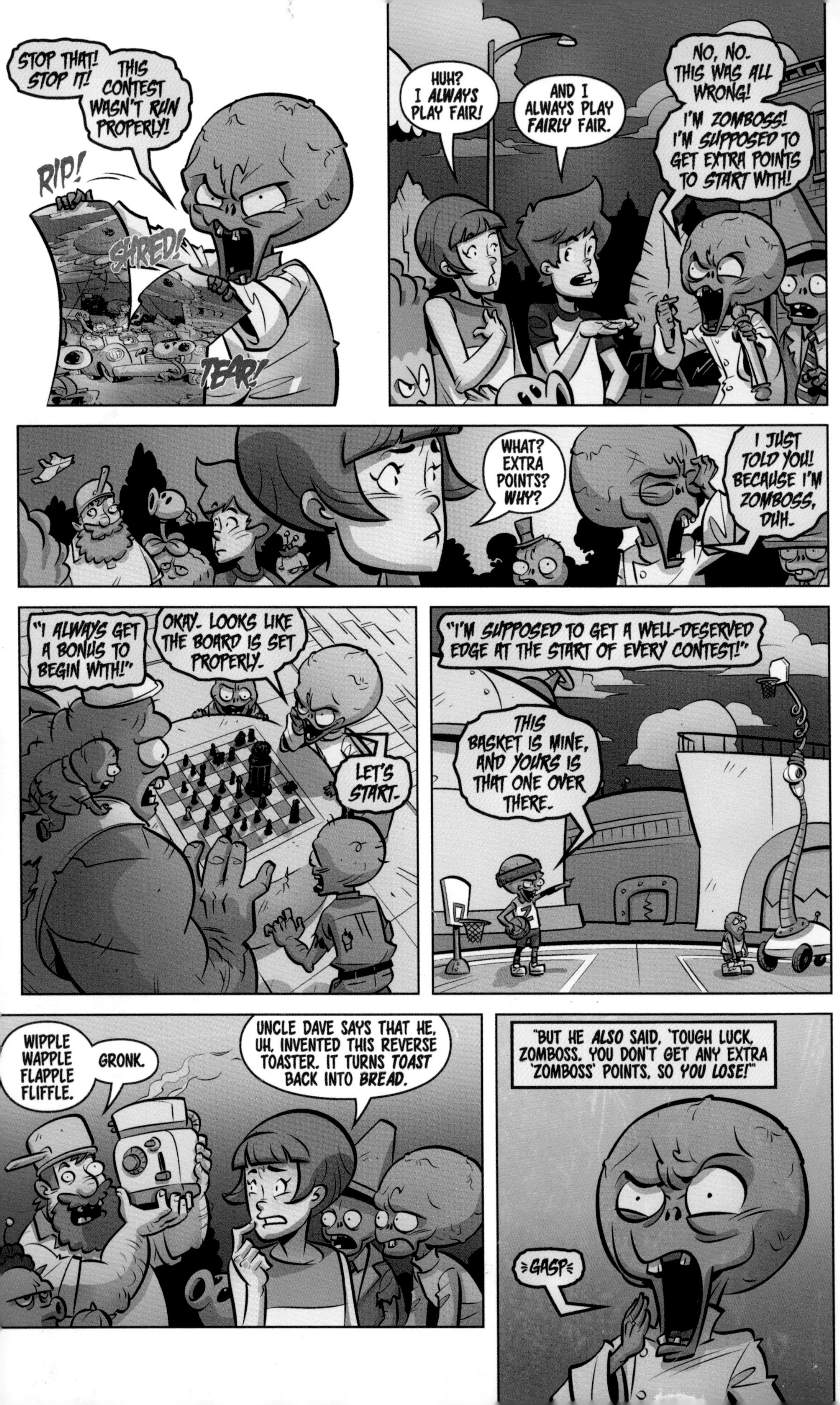
STOP THAT! STOP IT!
THIS CONTEST WASN'T RUN PROPERLY!
RIP!
SHRED!
TEAR!
HUH? I ALWAYS PLAY FAIR!
AND I ALWAYS PLAY FAIRLY FAIR.
NO, NO. THIS WAS ALL WRONG!
I'M ZOMBOSS! I'M SUPPOSED TO GET EXTRA POINTS TO START WITH!
WHAT? EXTRA POINTS? WHY?
I JUST TOLD YOU! BECAUSE I'M ZOMBOSS, DUH.
"I ALWAYS GET A BONUS TO BEGIN WITH!"
OKAY. LOOKS LIKE THE BOARD IS SET PROPERLY.
LET'S START.
"I'M SUPPOSED TO GET A WELL-DESERVED EDGE AT THE START OF EVERY CONTEST!"
THIS BASKET IS MINE, AND YOURS IS THAT ONE OVER THERE.
WIPPLE WAPPLE FLAPPLE FLIFFLE.
GRONK.
UNCLE DAVE SAYS THAT HE, UH, INVENTED THIS REVERSE TOASTER. IT TURNS TOAST BACK INTO BREAD.
"BUT HE ALSO SAID, 'TOUGH LUCK, ZOMBOSS. YOU DON'T GET ANY EXTRA 'ZOMBOSS' POINTS, SO YOU LOSE!"
GASP

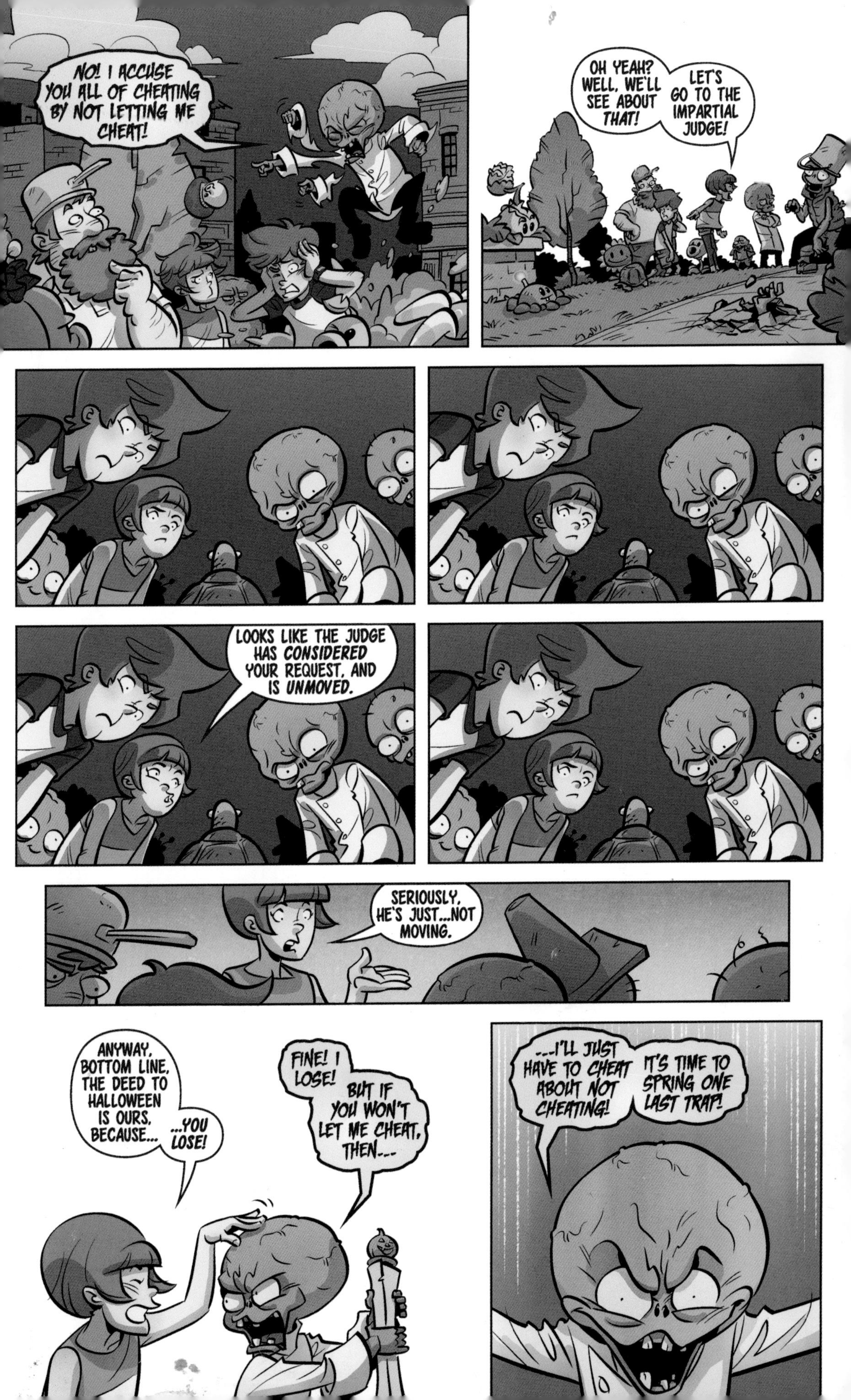
NO! I ACCUSE YOU ALL OF CHEATING BY NOT LETTING ME CHEAT!
OH YEAH? WELL, WE'LL SEE ABOUT THAT!
LET'S GO TO THE IMPARTIAL JUDGE!
LOOKS LIKE THE JUDGE HAS CONSIDERED YOUR REQUEST, AND IS UNMOVED.
SERIOUSLY, HE'S JUST...NOT MOVING.
ANYWAY, BOTTOM LINE, THE DEED TO HALLOWEEN IS OURS, BECAUSE...
...YOU LOSE!
FINE! I LOSE!
BUT IF YOU WON'T LET ME CHEAT, THEN...
...I'LL JUST HAVE TO CHEAT ABOUT NOT CHEATING!
IT'S TIME TO SPRING ONE LAST TRAP!

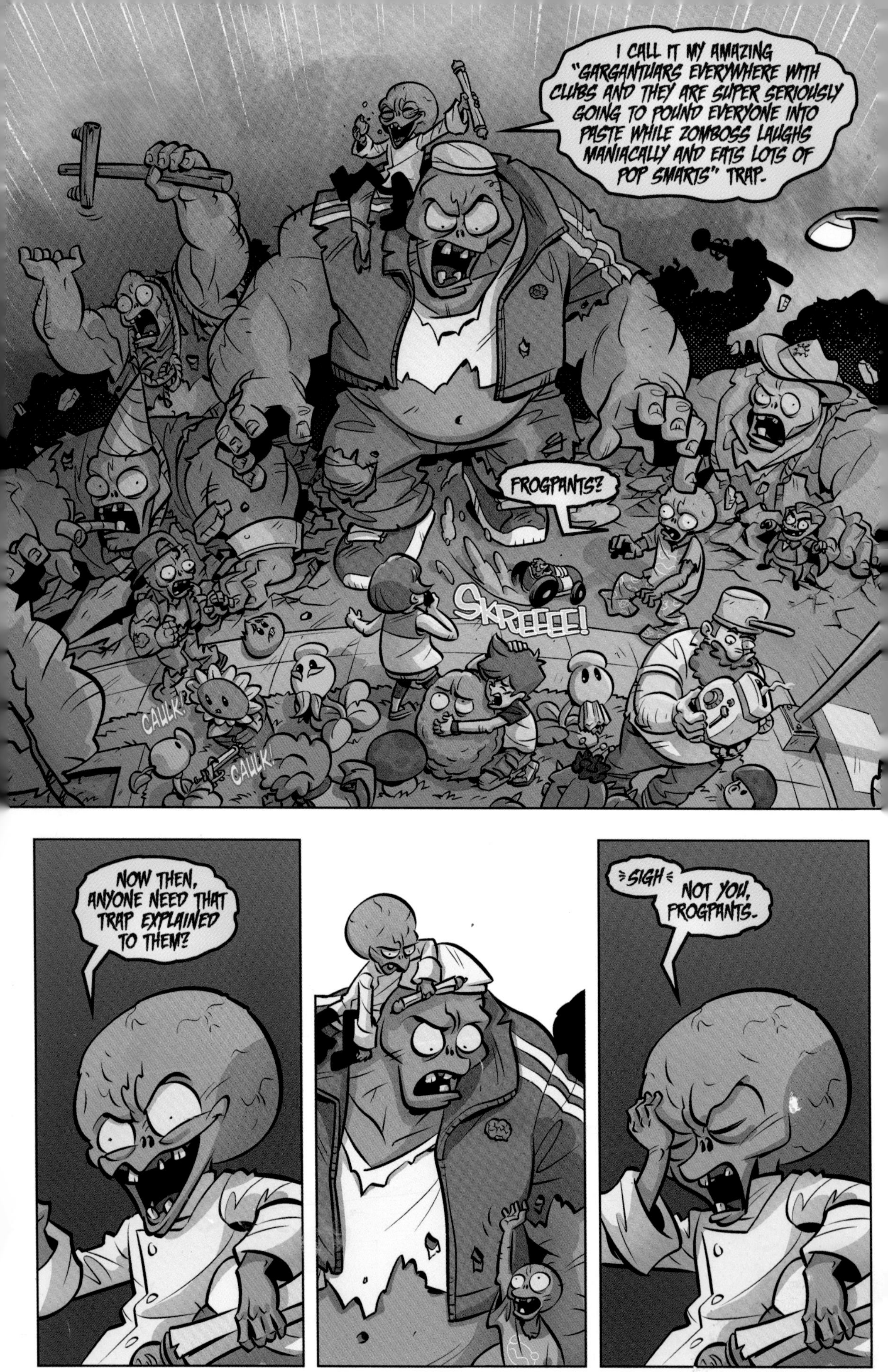
I CALL IT MY AMAZING "GARGANTUARS EVERYWHERE WITH CLUBS AND THEY ARE SUPER SERIOUSLY GOING TO POUND EVERYONE INTO PASTE WHILE ZOMBOSS LAUGHS MANIACALLY AND EATS LOTS OF POP SMARTS" TRAP.
FROGPANTS?
SKREEEEE!
CAULK!
CAULK!
NOW THEN, ANYONE NEED THAT TRAP EXPLAINED TO THEM?
SIGH
NOT YOU, FROGPANTS.

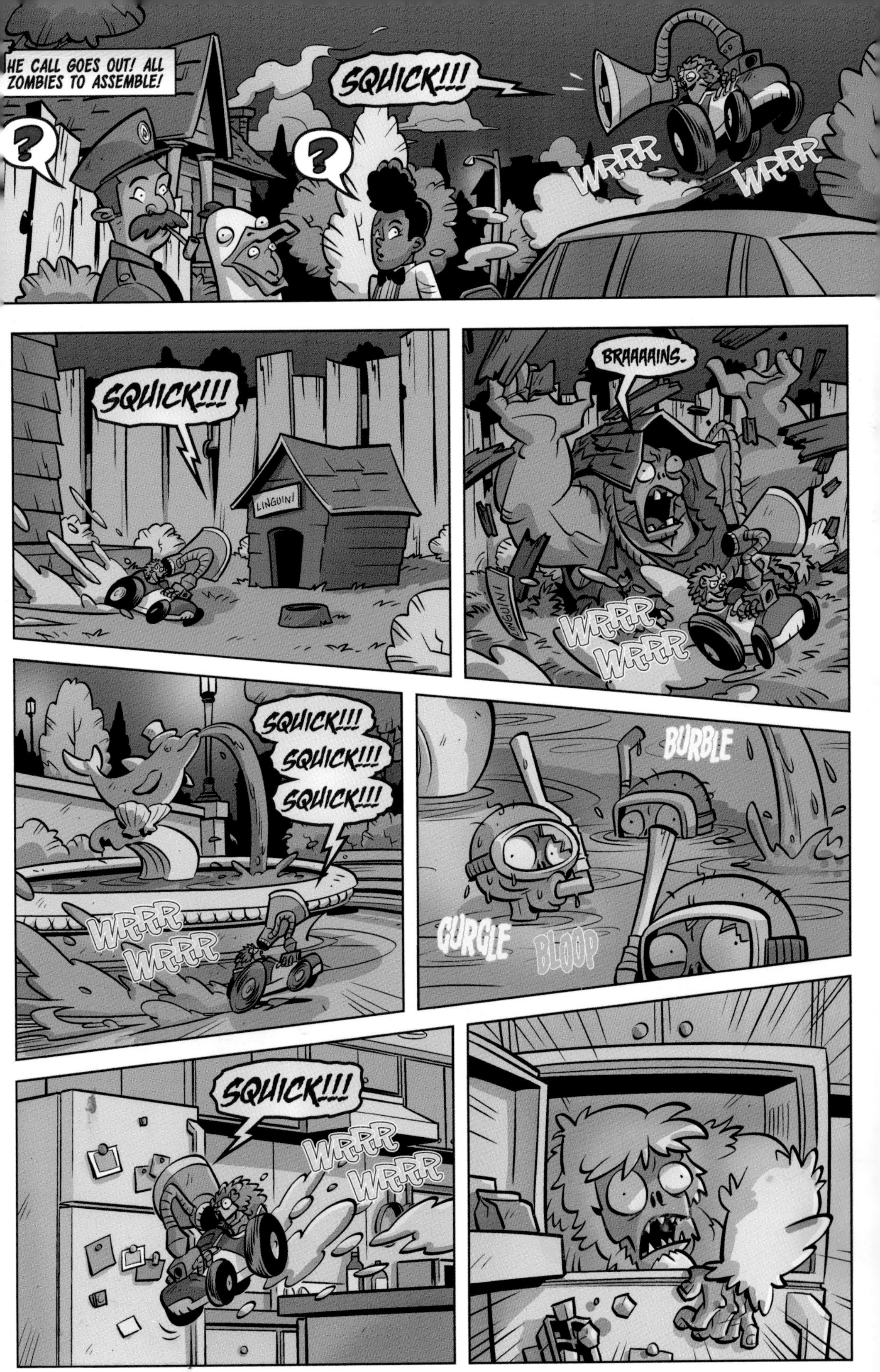
HE CALL GOES OUT! ALL ZOMBIES TO ASSEMBLE!
?
?
SQUICK!!!
WRRRR
WRRRR
SQUICK!!!
LINGUINI
BRAAAAAINS.
LINGUINI
WRRRR
WRRRR
SQUICK!!!
SQUICK!!!
SQUICK!!!
WRRRR
WRRRR
BURBLE
GURGLE
BLOOP
SQUICK!!!
WRRRR
WRRRR

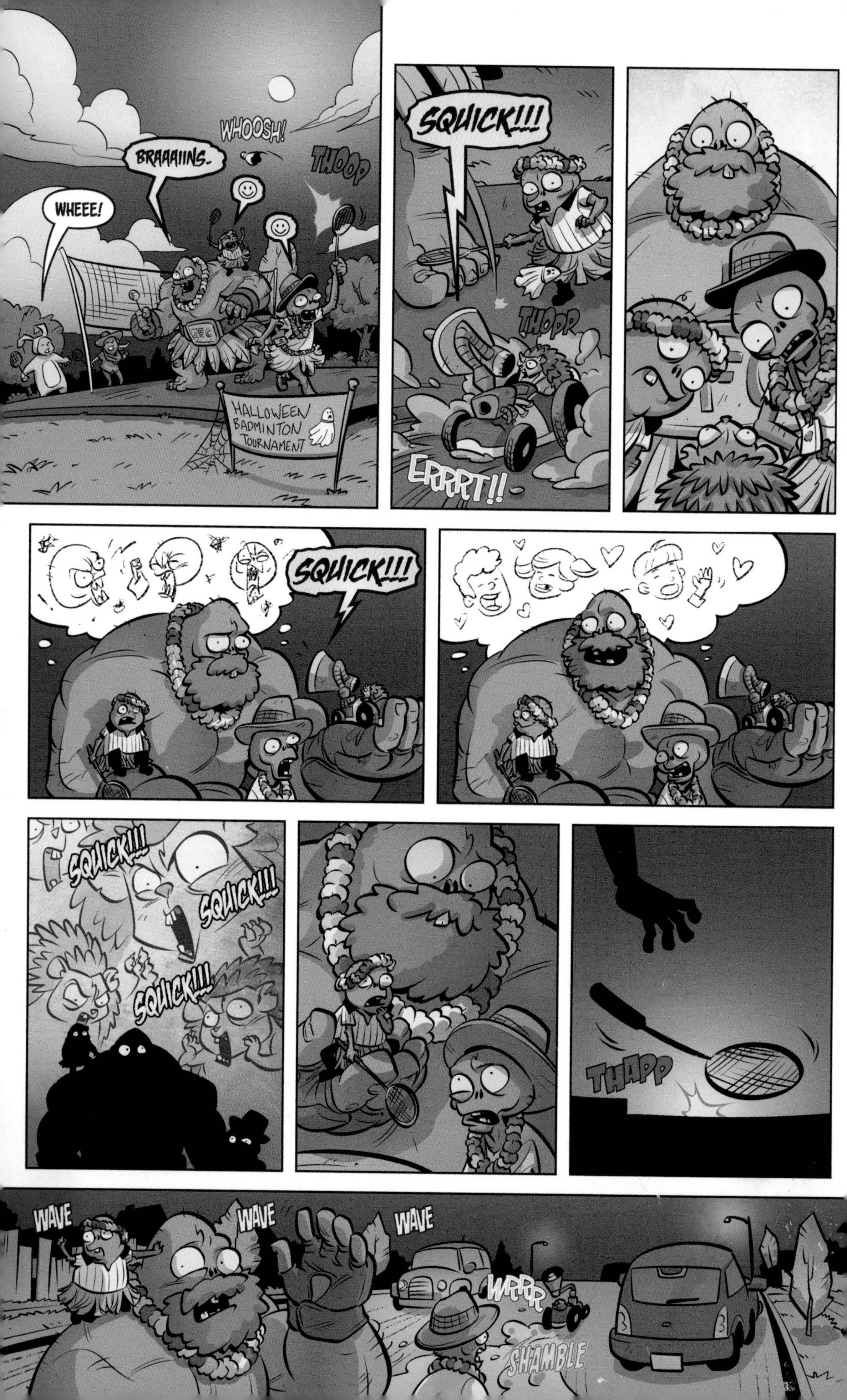
WHOOSH!
BRAAAAIINS.
WHEEE!
THOOP
HALLOWEEN BADMINTON TOURNAMENT
SQUICK!!!!
THOPP
ERRRT!!
SQUICK!!!
SQUICK!!!
SQUICK!!!
SQUICK!!!
THAPP
WAVE
WAVE
WAVE
WRRR
SHAMBLE

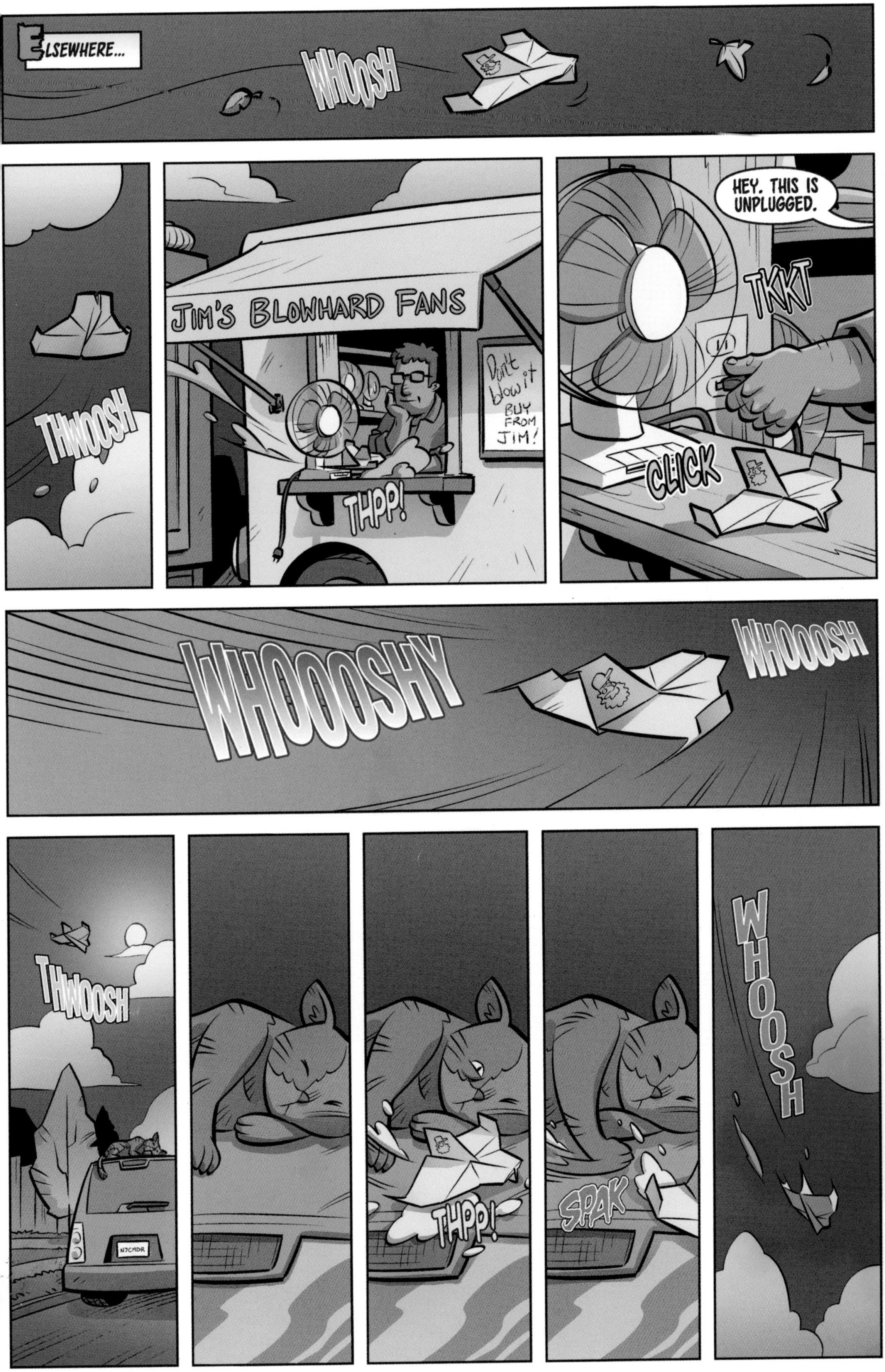
ELSEWHERE...
WHOOSH
THWOOSH
JIM'S BLOWHARD FANS
Don't blow it
BUY FROM JIM!
THPP!
HEY. THIS IS UNPLUGGED.
TKKT
CLICK
WHOOOOSHY
WHOOOSH
THWOOSH
N7CMDR
THPP!
SPAK
WHOOOSH

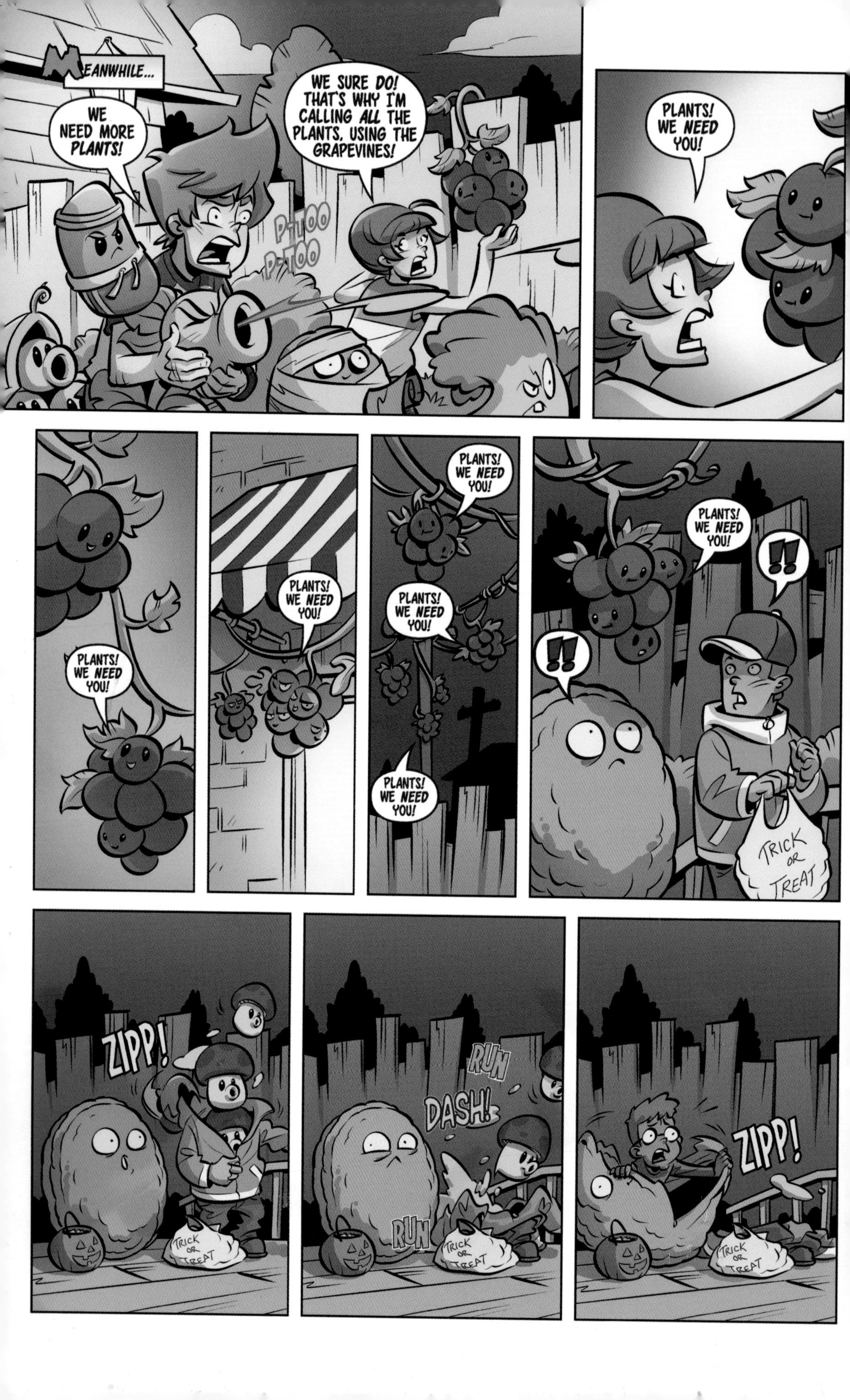
MEANWHILE...
WE NEED MORE PLANTS!
WE SURE DO! THAT'S WHY I'M CALLING ALL THE PLANTS, USING THE GRAPEVINES!
P-TOO
P-TOO
PLANTS! WE NEED YOU!
PLANTS! WE NEED YOU!
PLANTS! WE NEED YOU!
PLANTS! WE NEED YOU!
PLANTS! WE NEED YOU!
PLANTS! WE NEED YOU!
PLANTS! WE NEED YOU!
!!
!!
TRICK OR TREAT
ZIPP!
TRICK OR TREAT
RUN
DASH!
RUN
TRICK OR TREAT
ZIPP!
TRICK OR TREAT

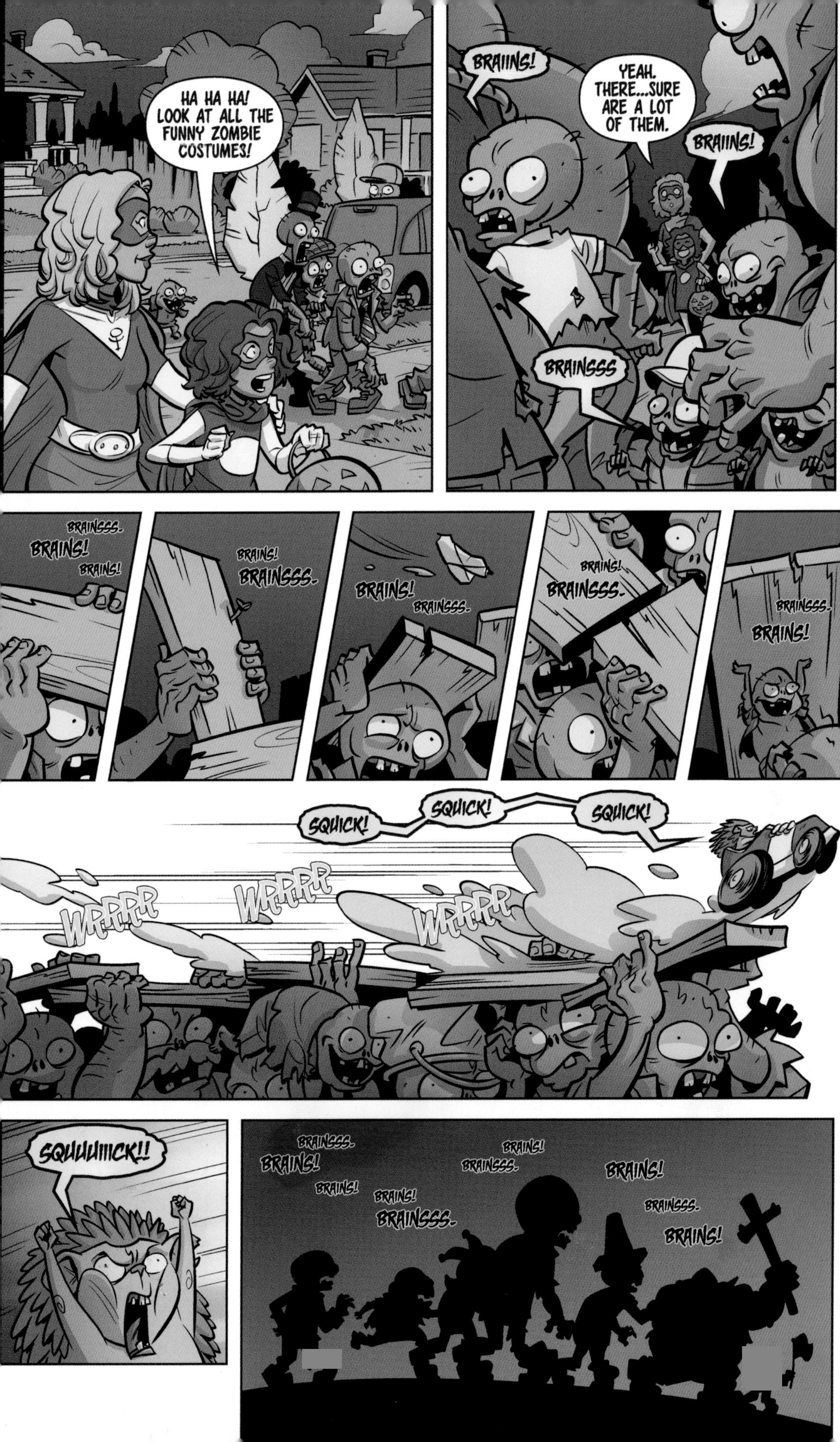
HA HA HA! LOOK AT ALL THE FUNNY ZOMBIE COSTUMES!
BRAIINS!
YEAH. THERE...SURE ARE A LOT OF THEM.
BRAIINS!
BRAINSSS
BRAINSSS.
BRAINS!
BRAINS!
BRAINS!
BRAINSSS.
BRAINS!
BRAINSSS.
BRAINS!
BRAINSSS.
BRAINSSS.
BRAINS!
SQUICK!
SQUICK!
SQUICK!
WRRRR
WRRRR
WRRRR
SQUUUIIICK!!
BRAINSSS.
BRAINS!
BRAINS!
BRAINS!
BRAINSSS.
BRAINS!
BRAINSSS.
BRAINS!
BRAINSSS.
BRAINS!

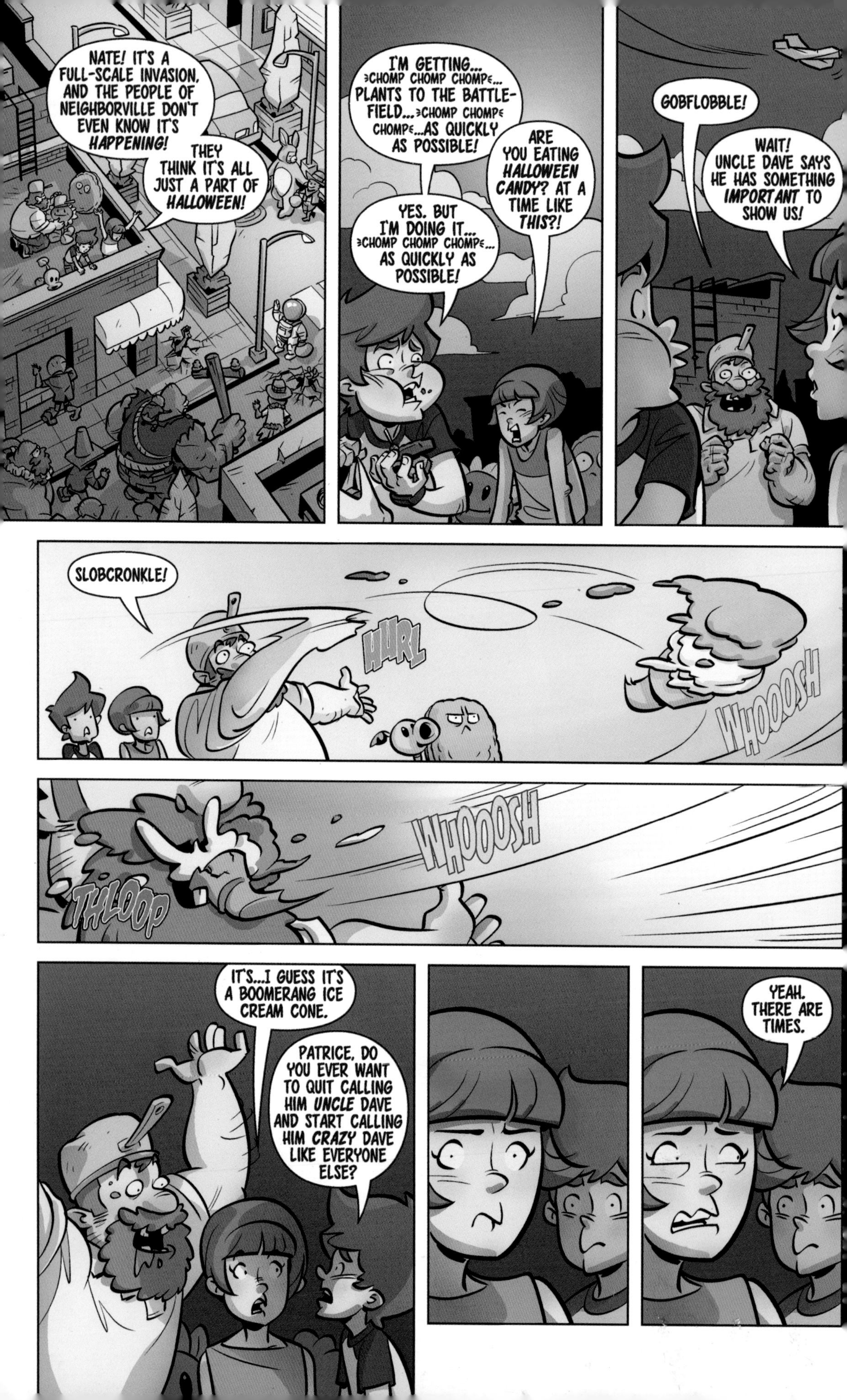
NATE! IT'S A FULL-SCALE INVASION, AND THE PEOPLE OF NEIGHBORVILLE DON'T EVEN KNOW IT'S HAPPENING!
THEY THINK IT'S ALL JUST A PART OF HALLOWEEN!
I'M GETTING... ≥CHOMP CHOMP CHOMP≤... PLANTS TO THE BATTLE-FIELD... ≥CHOMP CHOMP CHOMP≤...AS QUICKLY AS POSSIBLE!
ARE YOU EATING HALLOWEEN CANDY? AT A TIME LIKE THIS?!
YES. BUT I'M DOING IT... ≥CHOMP CHOMP CHOMP≤... AS QUICKLY AS POSSIBLE!
GOBFLOBBLE!
WAIT! UNCLE DAVE SAYS HE HAS SOMETHING IMPORTANT TO SHOW US!
SLOBCRONKLE!
HURL
WHOOOSH
WHOOOSH
THLOOP
IT'S...I GUESS IT'S A BOOMERANG ICE CREAM CONE.
PATRICE, DO YOU EVER WANT TO QUIT CALLING HIM UNCLE DAVE AND START CALLING HIM CRAZY DAVE LIKE EVERYONE ELSE?
YEAH. THERE ARE TIMES.

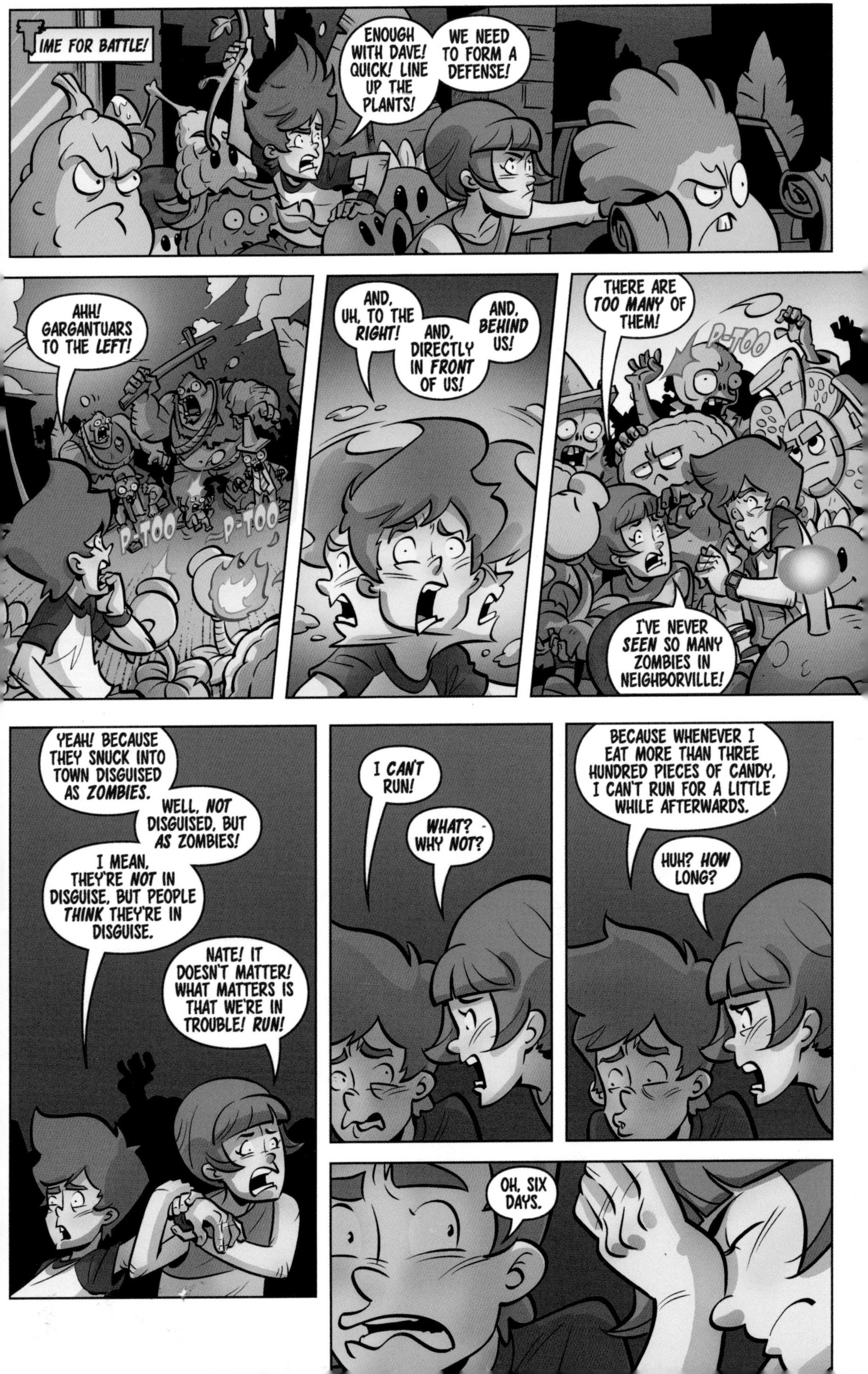
TIME FOR BATTLE!
ENOUGH WITH DAVE! QUICK! LINE UP THE PLANTS!
WE NEED TO FORM A DEFENSE!
AHH! GARGANTUARS TO THE LEFT!
P-TOO
P-TOO
AND, UH, TO THE RIGHT!
AND, DIRECTLY IN FRONT OF US!
AND, BEHIND US!
THERE ARE TOO MANY OF THEM!
P-TOO
I'VE NEVER SEEN SO MANY ZOMBIES IN NEIGHBORVILLE!
YEAH! BECAUSE THEY SNUCK INTO TOWN DISGUISED AS ZOMBIES.
WELL, NOT DISGUISED, BUT AS ZOMBIES!
I MEAN, THEY'RE NOT IN DISGUISE, BUT PEOPLE THINK THEY'RE IN DISGUISE.
NATE! IT DOESN'T MATTER! WHAT MATTERS IS THAT WE'RE IN TROUBLE! RUN!
I CAN'T RUN!
WHAT? WHY NOT?
BECAUSE WHENEVER I EAT MORE THAN THREE HUNDRED PIECES OF CANDY, I CAN'T RUN FOR A LITTLE WHILE AFTERWARDS.
HUH? HOW LONG?
OH, SIX DAYS.

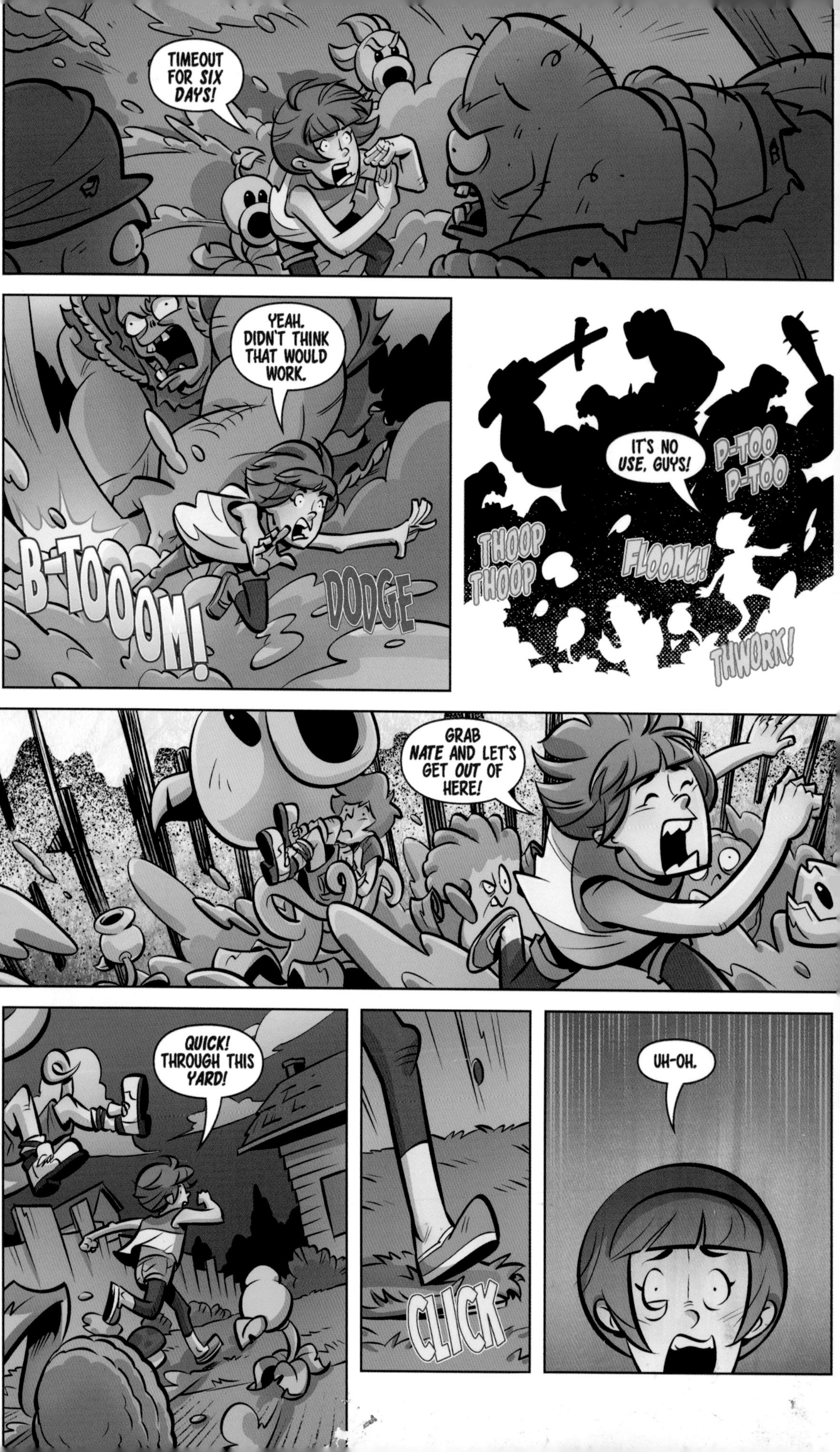
TIMEOUT FOR SIX DAYS!
YEAH. DIDN'T THINK THAT WOULD WORK.
B-TOOOOM!
DODGE
IT'S NO USE, GUYS!
P-TOO P-TOO
THOOP THOOP
FLOONG!
THWORK!
GRAB NATE AND LET'S GET OUT OF HERE!
QUICK! THROUGH THIS YARD!
CLICK
UH-OH.

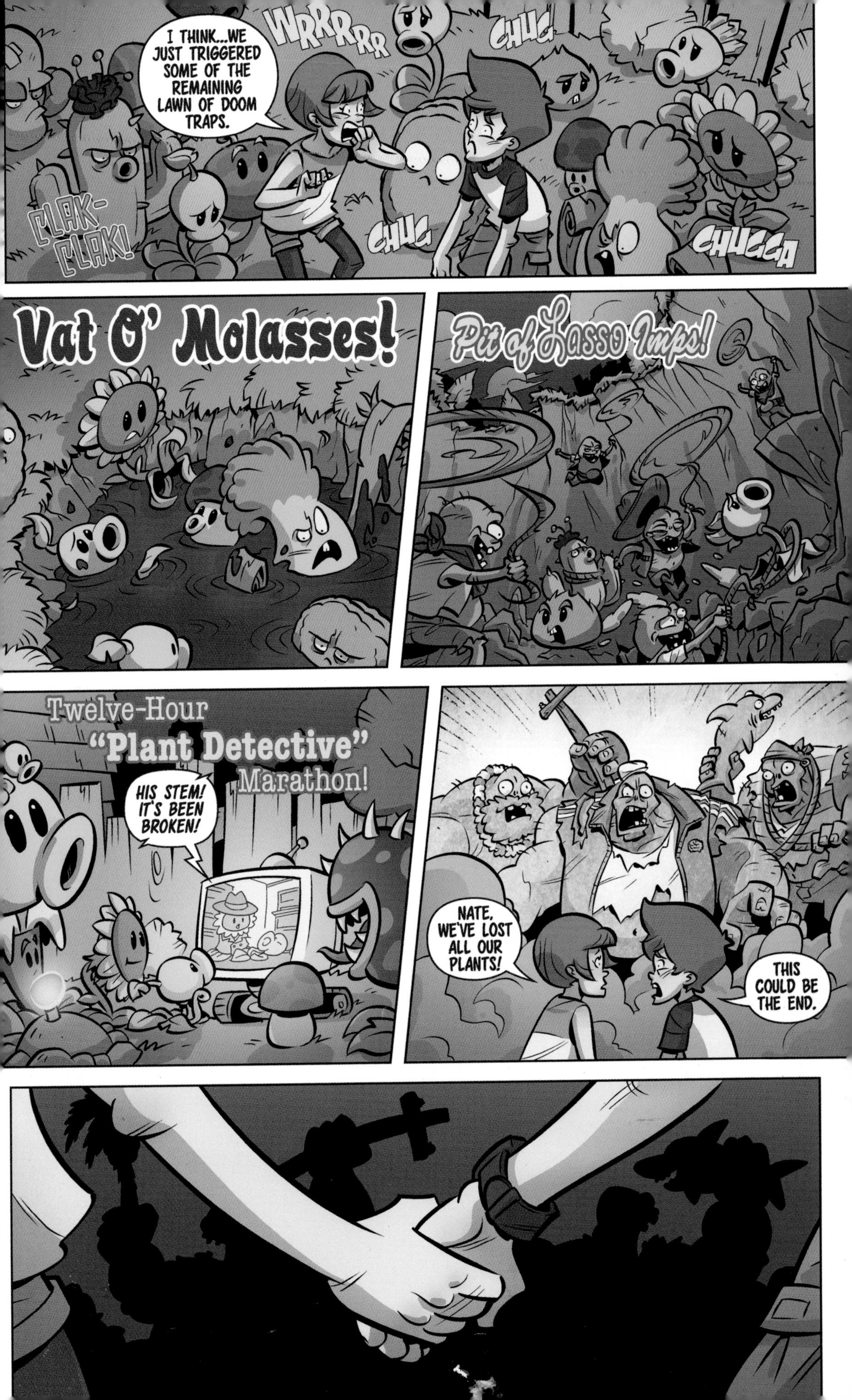
WRRRRRR
CHUG
I THINK...WE JUST TRIGGERED SOME OF THE REMAINING LAWN OF DOOM TRAPS.
CLAK-CLAK!
CHUG
CHUGGA
Vat O' Molasses!
Pit of Lasso Imps!
Twelve-Hour "Plant Detective" Marathon!
HIS STEM! IT'S BEEN BROKEN!
NATE, WE'VE LOST ALL OUR PLANTS!
THIS COULD BE THE END.

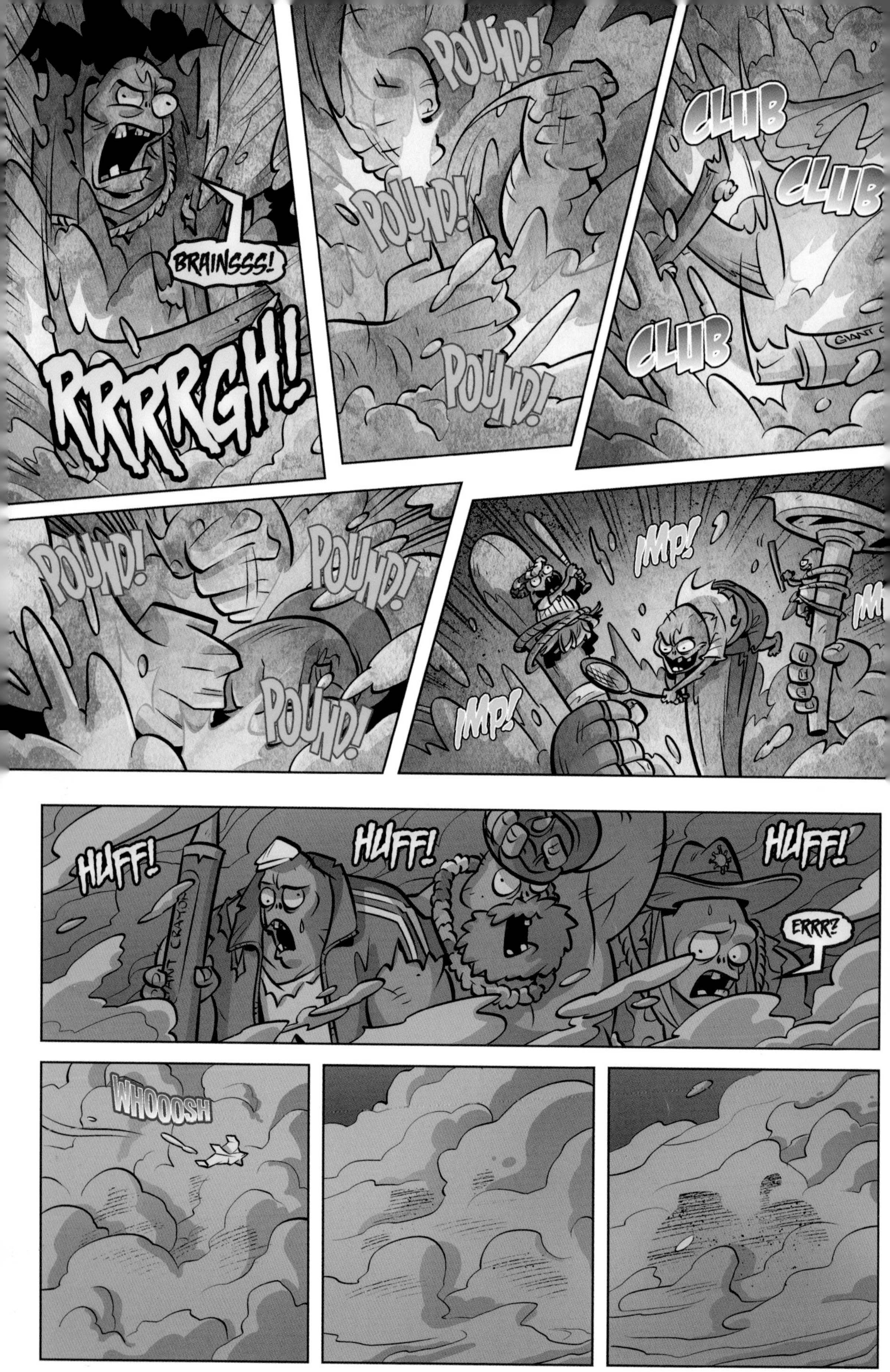
BRAINSSS!
RRRRGH!
POUND!
POUND!
POUND!
CLUB
CLUB
CLUB
POUND!
POUND!
POUND!
IMP!
IMP!
HUFF!
HUFF!
HUFF!
ERRR?
WHOOOSH

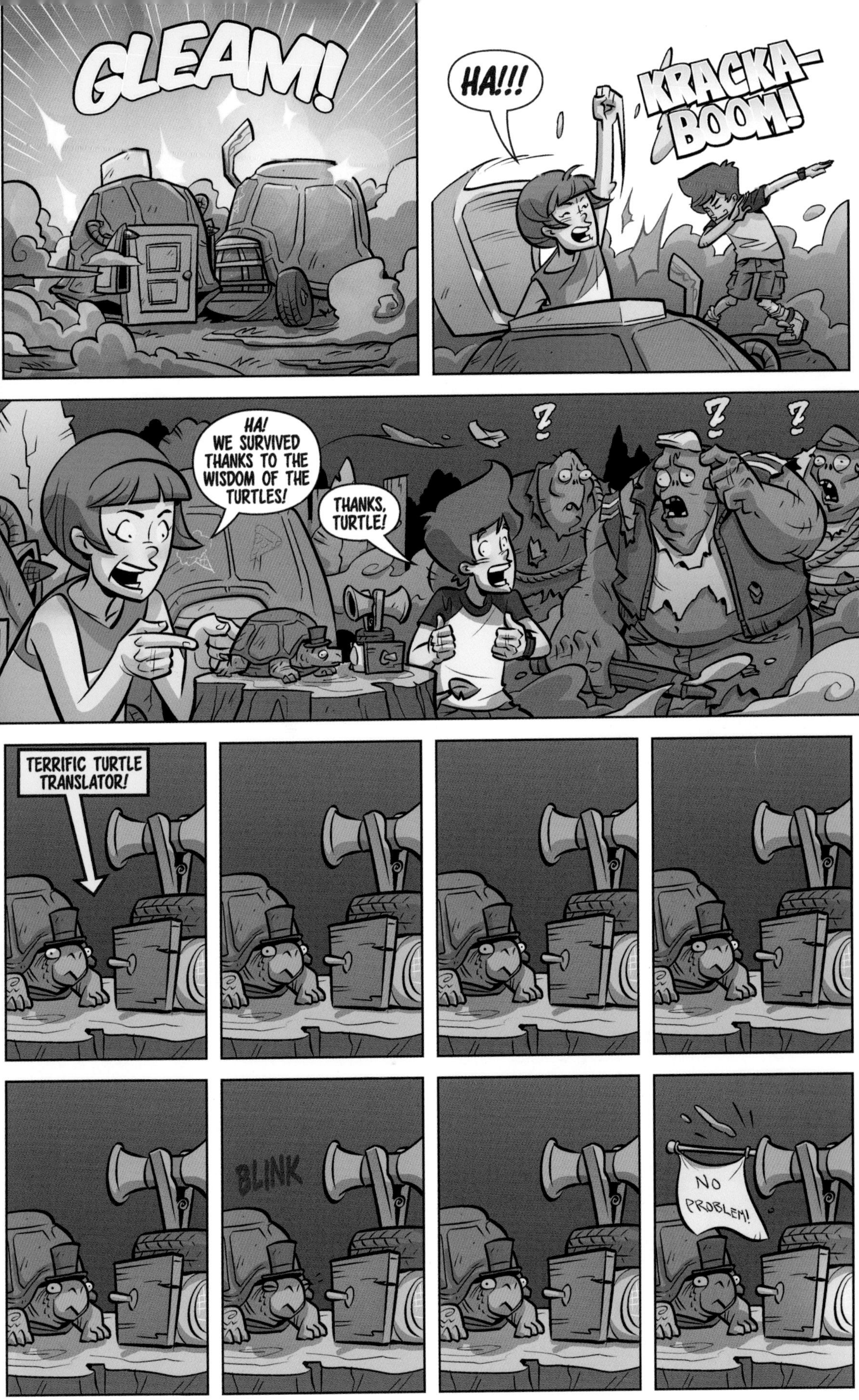
GLEAM!
HA!!!
KRACKA-BOOM!
HA! WE SURVIVED THANKS TO THE WISDOM OF THE TURTLES!
THANKS, TURTLE!
TERRIFIC TURTLE TRANSLATOR!
BLINK
NO PROBLEM!

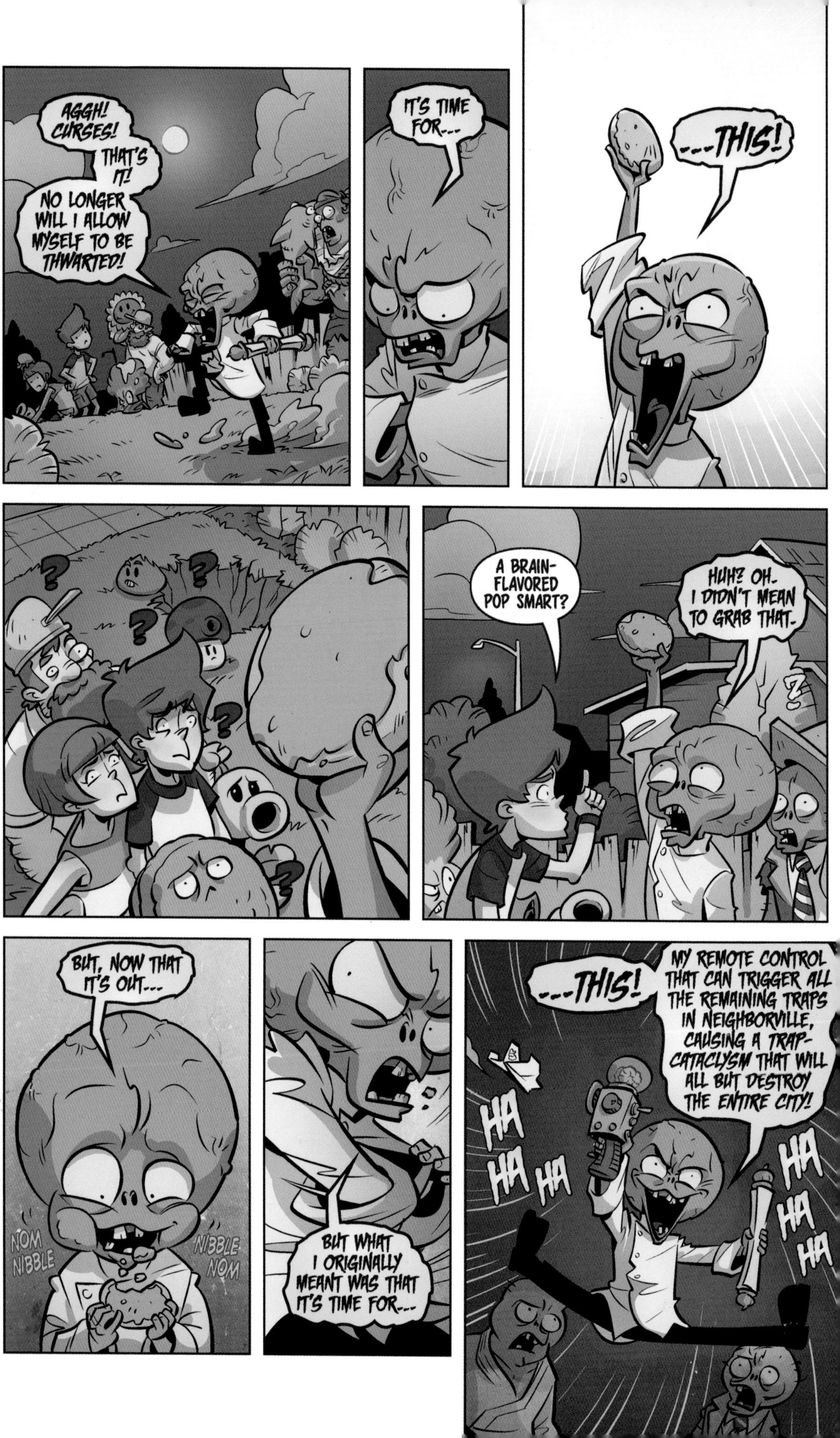
AGGH! CURSES!
THAT'S IT!
NO LONGER WILL I ALLOW MYSELF TO BE THWARTED!
IT'S TIME FOR...
...THIS!
A BRAIN-FLAVORED POP SMART?
HUH? OH. I DIDN'T MEAN TO GRAB THAT.
BUT, NOW THAT IT'S OUT...
NOM NIBBLE
NIBBLE NOM
BUT WHAT I ORIGINALLY MEANT WAS THAT IT'S TIME FOR...
...THIS!
MY REMOTE CONTROL THAT CAN TRIGGER ALL THE REMAINING TRAPS IN NEIGHBORVILLE, CAUSING A TRAP-CATACLYSM THAT WILL ALL BUT DESTROY THE ENTIRE CITY!
HA HA HA
HA HA HA

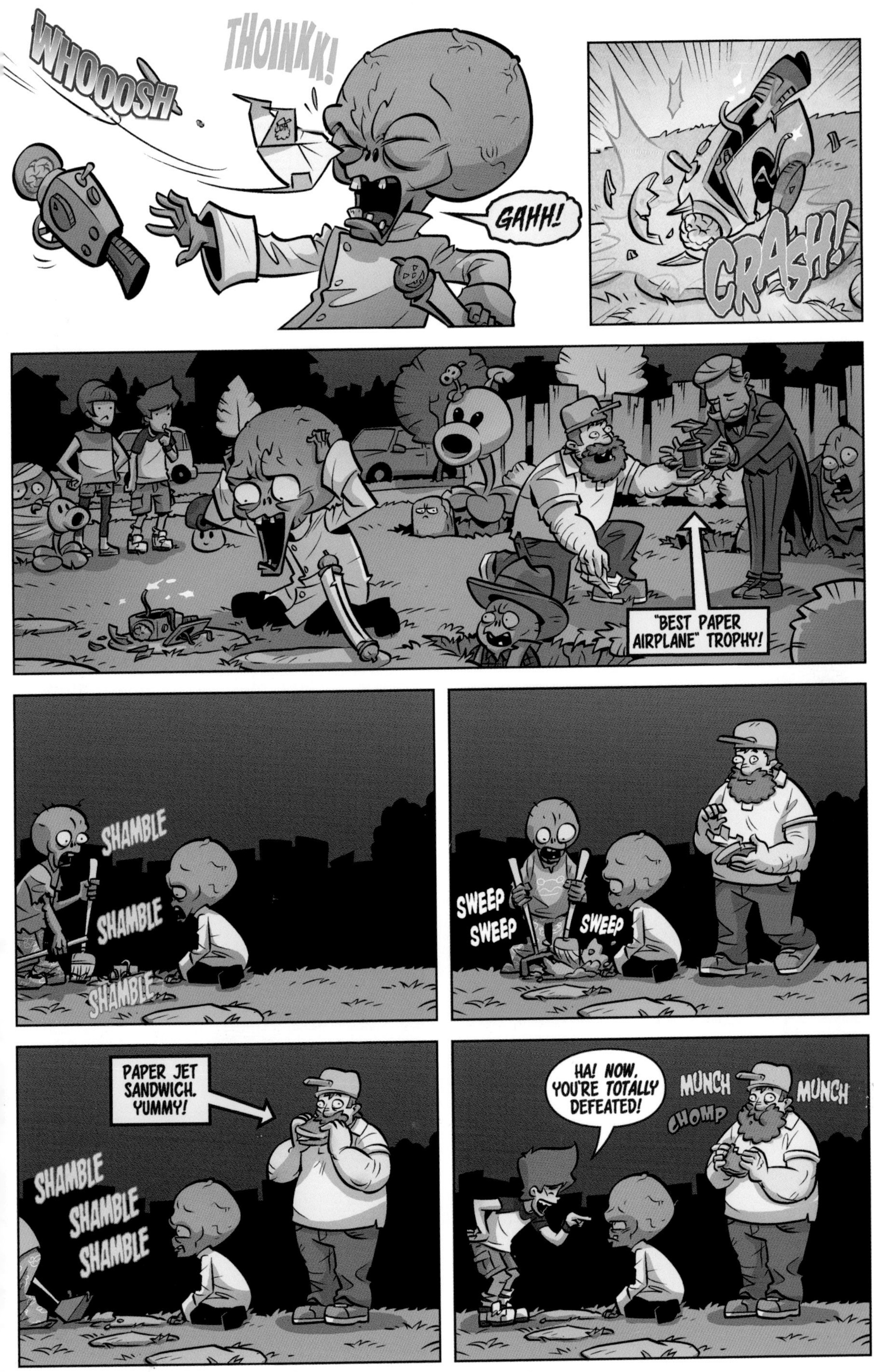
WHOOOOSH
THOINKK!
GAHH!
CRASH!
"BEST PAPER AIRPLANE" TROPHY!
SHAMBLE
SHAMBLE
SHAMBLE
SWEEP
SWEEP
SWEEP
PAPER JET SANDWICH. YUMMY!
SHAMBLE
SHAMBLE
SHAMBLE
HA! NOW, YOU'RE TOTALLY DEFEATED!
MUNCH
CHOMP
MUNCH

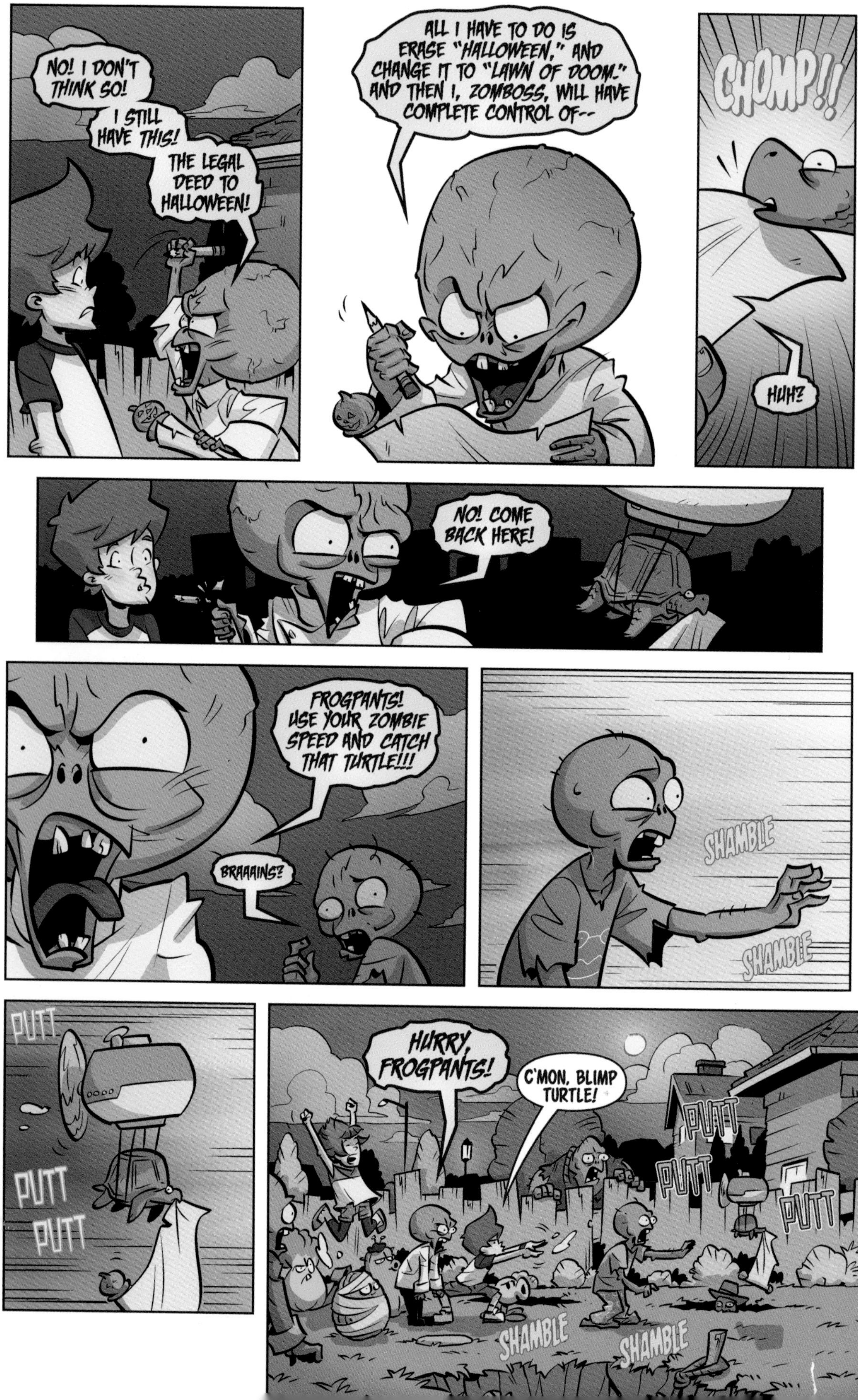
NO! I DON'T THINK SO!
I STILL HAVE THIS!
THE LEGAL DEED TO HALLOWEEN!
ALL I HAVE TO DO IS ERASE "HALLOWEEN," AND CHANGE IT TO "LAWN OF DOOM." AND THEN I, ZOMBOSS, WILL HAVE COMPLETE CONTROL OF--
CHOMP!!
HUH?
NO! COME BACK HERE!
FROGPANTS! USE YOUR ZOMBIE SPEED AND CATCH THAT TURTLE!!!
BRAAAINS?
SHAMBLE
SHAMBLE
PUTT
PUTT
PUTT
HURRY, FROGPANTS!
C'MON, BLIMP TURTLE!
PUTT
PUTT
PUTT
SHAMBLE
SHAMBLE

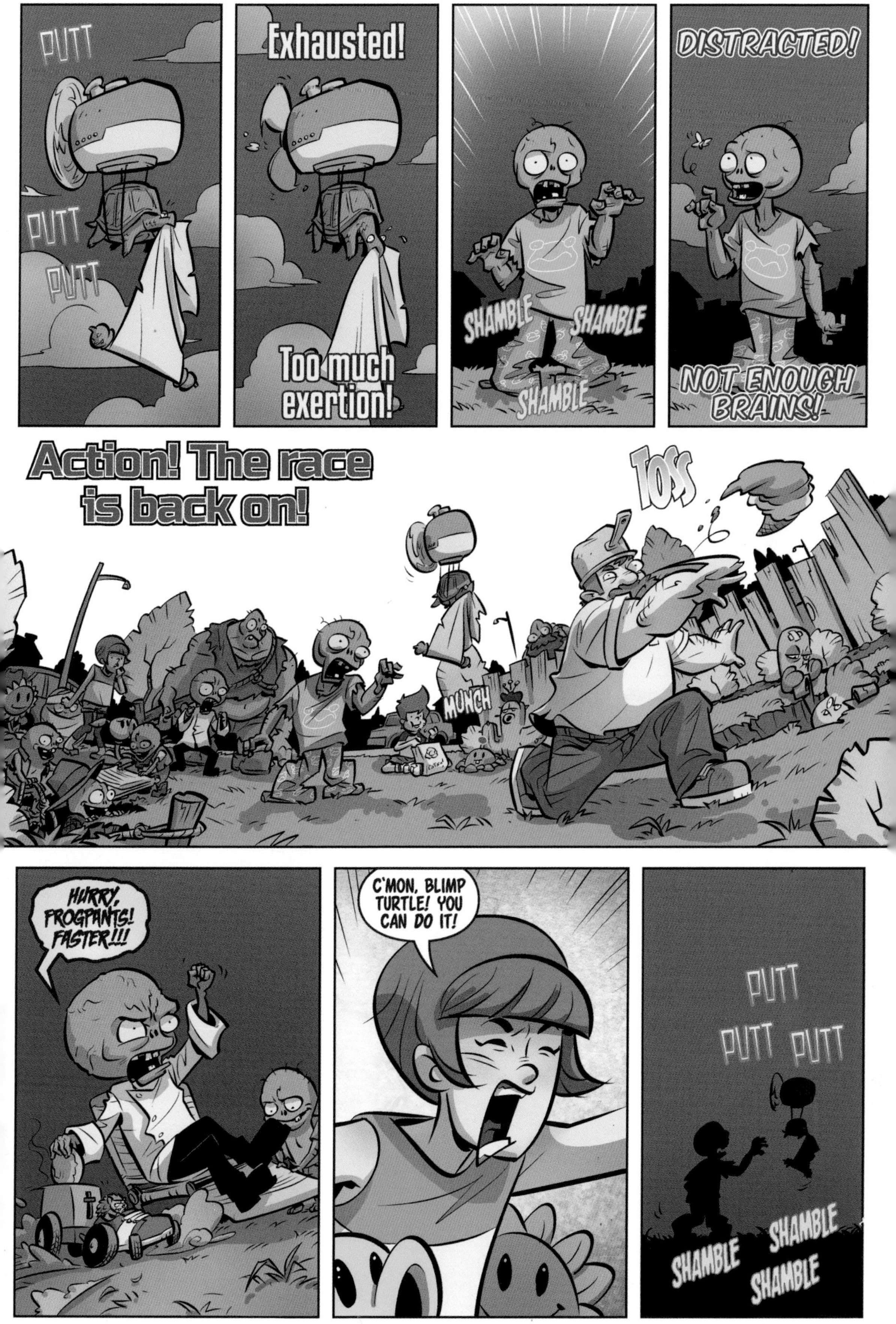
PUTT
PUTT
PUTT
Exhausted!
Too much exertion!
SHAMBLE
SHAMBLE
SHAMBLE
DISTRACTED!
NOT ENOUGH BRAINS!
Action! The race is back on!
TOSS
MUNCH
HURRY, FROGPANTS! FASTER!!!
C'MON, BLIMP TURTLE! YOU CAN DO IT!
PUTT
PUTT PUTT
SHAMBLE
SHAMBLE
SHAMBLE

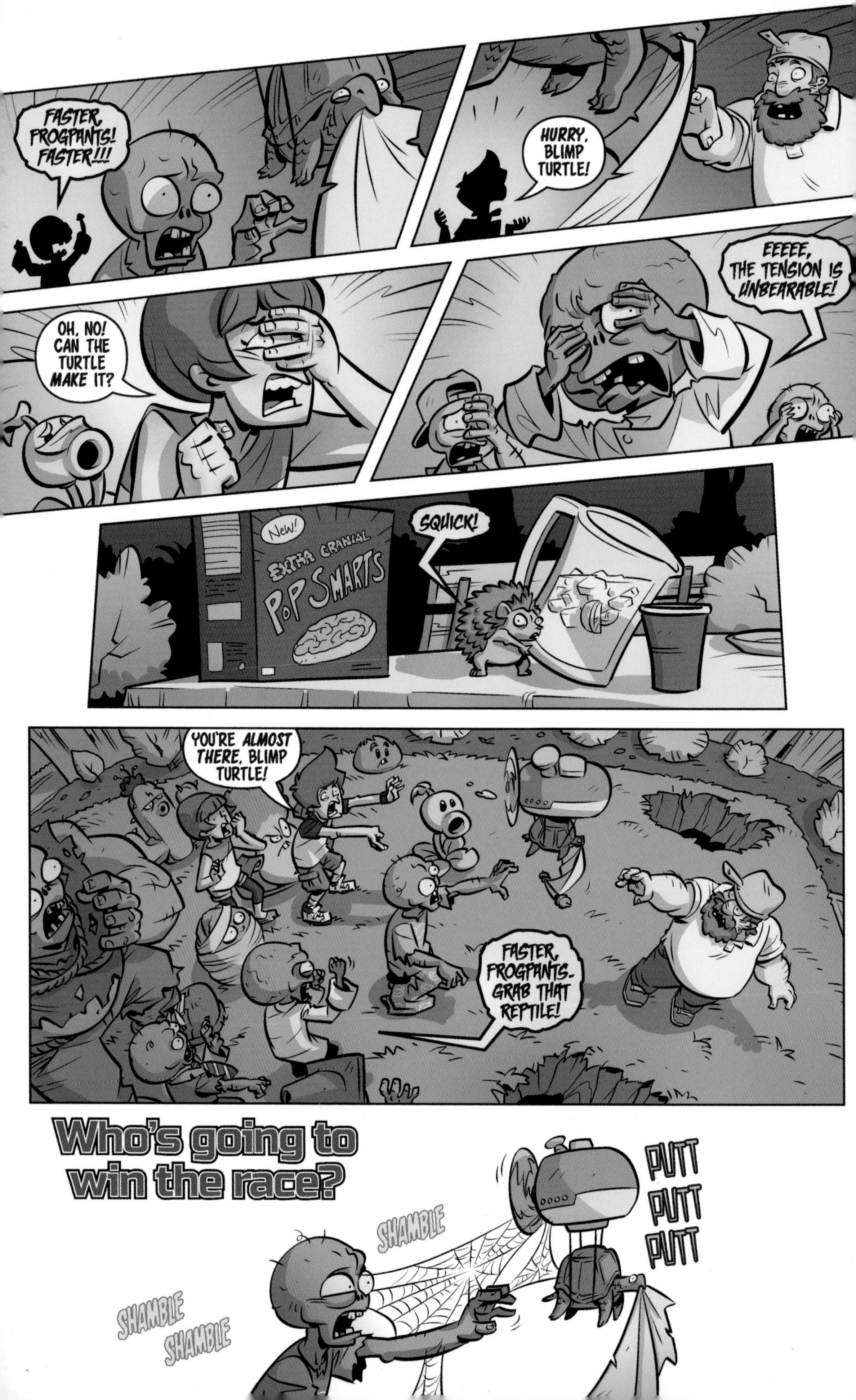
FASTER, FROGPANTS! FASTER!!!
HURRY, BLIMP TURTLE!
OH, NO! CAN THE TURTLE MAKE IT?
EEEEE, THE TENSION IS UNBEARABLE!
New!
EXTRA CRANIAL
POP SMARTS
SQUICK!
YOU'RE ALMOST THERE, BLIMP TURTLE!
FASTER, FROGPANTS. GRAB THAT REPTILE!
Who's going to win the race?
SHAMBLE
SHAMBLE
SHAMBLE
PUTT
PUTT
PUTT

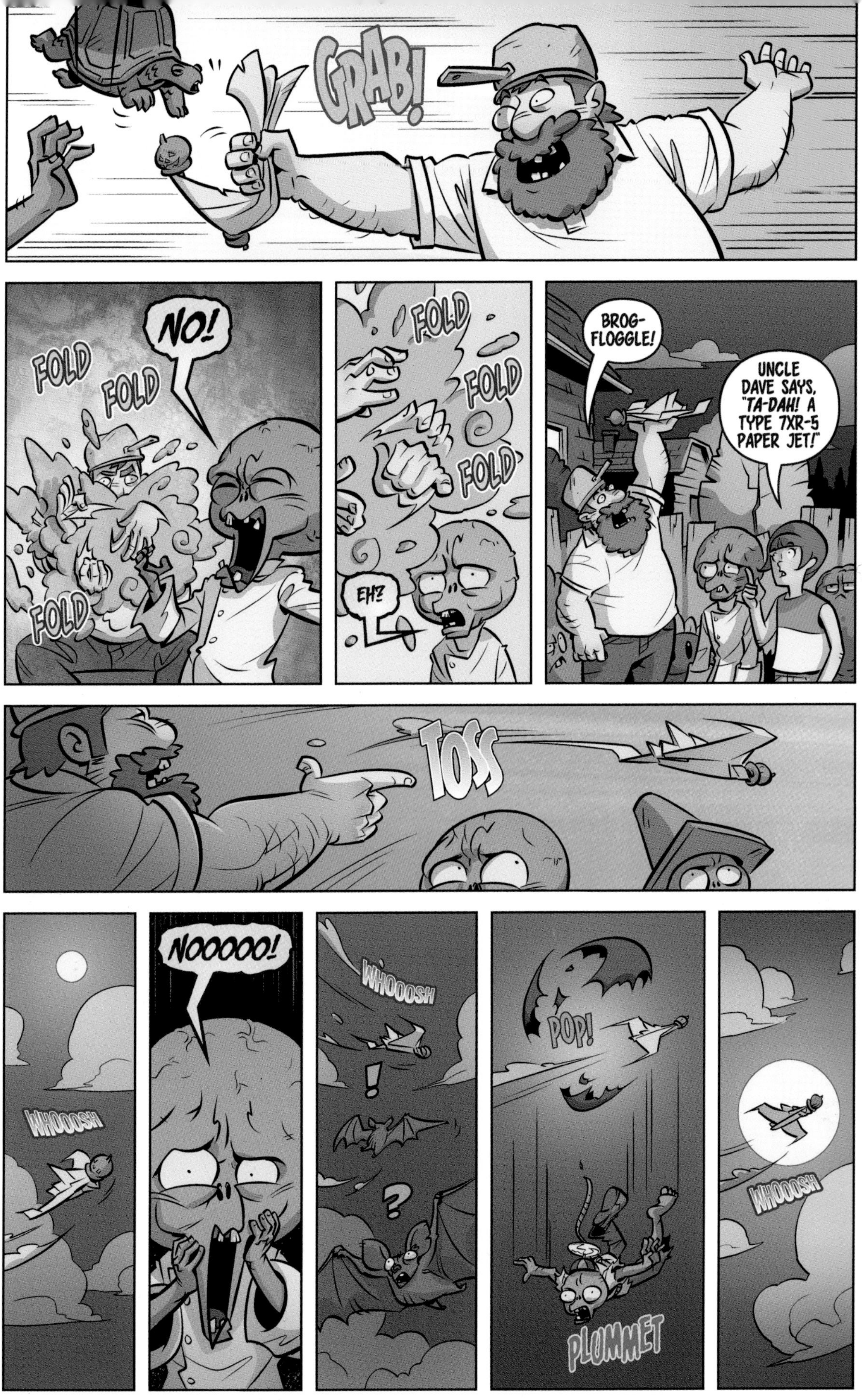
GRAB!
FOLD
FOLD
NO!
FOLD
FOLD
FOLD
FOLD
EH?
BROG-FLOGGLE!
UNCLE DAVE SAYS, "TA-DAH! A TYPE 7XR-5 PAPER JET!"
TOSS
WHOOOSH
NOOOOO!
WHOOOSH
!
?
POP!
PLUMMET
WHOOOSH

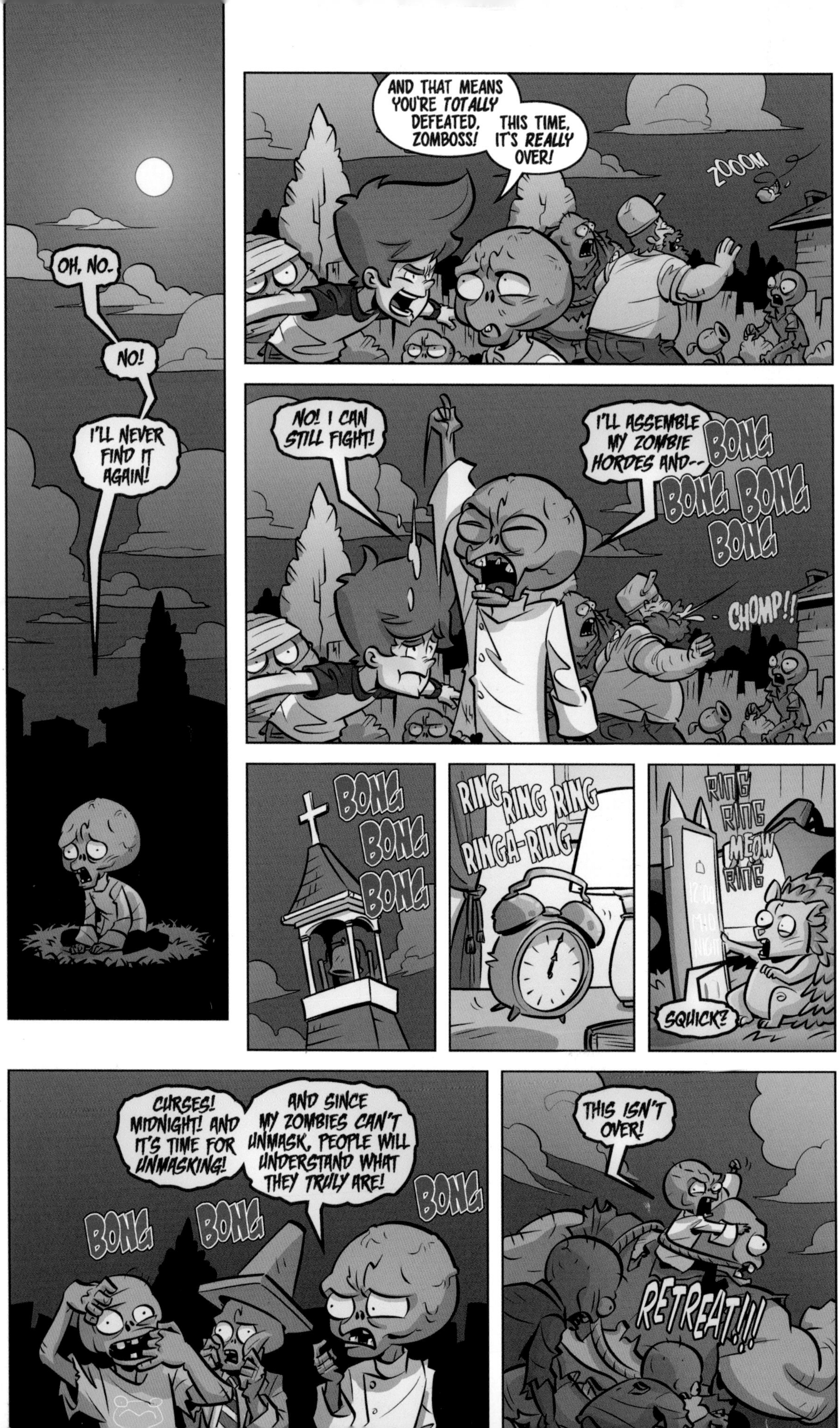
OH, NO...
NO!
I'LL NEVER FIND IT AGAIN!
AND THAT MEANS YOU'RE TOTALLY DEFEATED, ZOMBOSS!
THIS TIME, IT'S REALLY OVER!
ZOOOM
NO! I CAN STILL FIGHT!
I'LL ASSEMBLE MY ZOMBIE HORDES AND--
BONG
BONG BONG
BONG
CHOMP!!
BONG
BONG
BONG
RING RING RING
RINGA-RING
RING
RING
MEOW
RING
SQUICK?
CURSES! MIDNIGHT! AND IT'S TIME FOR UNMASKING!
AND SINCE MY ZOMBIES CAN'T UNMASK, PEOPLE WILL UNDERSTAND WHAT THEY TRULY ARE!
BONG
BONG
BONG
THIS ISN'T OVER!
RETREAT!!!

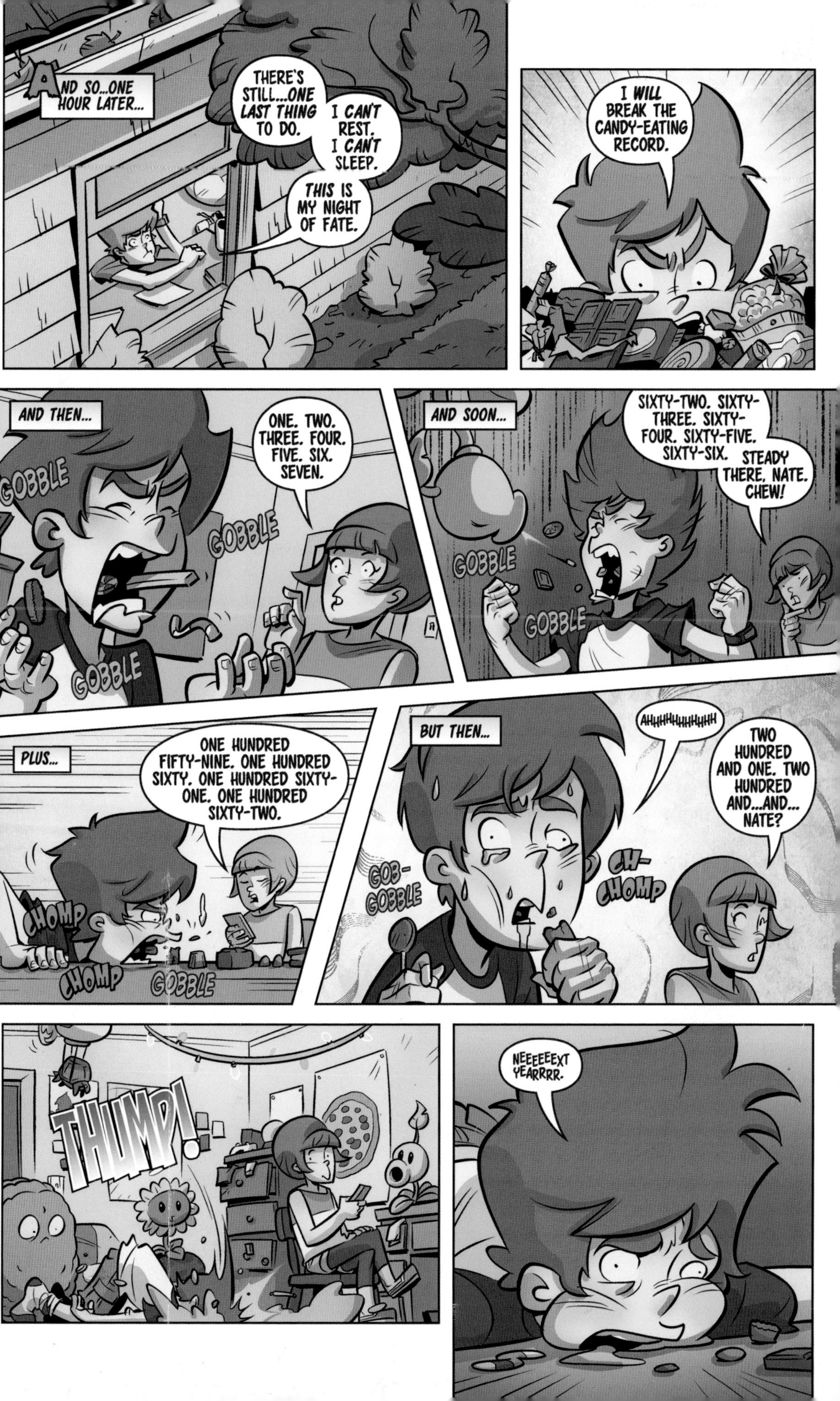
AND SO...ONE HOUR LATER...
THERE'S STILL...ONE LAST THING TO DO.
I CAN'T REST. I CAN'T SLEEP.
THIS IS MY NIGHT OF FATE.
I WILL BREAK THE CANDY-EATING RECORD.
AND THEN...
ONE. TWO. THREE. FOUR. FIVE. SIX. SEVEN.
GOBBLE
GOBBLE
GOBBLE
AND SOON...
SIXTY-TWO. SIXTY-THREE. SIXTY-FOUR. SIXTY-FIVE. SIXTY-SIX.
STEADY THERE, NATE. CHEW!
GOBBLE
GOBBLE
PLUS...
ONE HUNDRED FIFTY-NINE. ONE HUNDRED SIXTY. ONE HUNDRED SIXTY-ONE. ONE HUNDRED SIXTY-TWO.
CHOMP
CHOMP
GOBBLE
BUT THEN...
AHHHHHHHHHHH
TWO HUNDRED AND ONE. TWO HUNDRED AND...AND... NATE?
GOB-GOBBLE
CH-CHOMP
THUMP!
NEEEEEEXT YEARRRR.

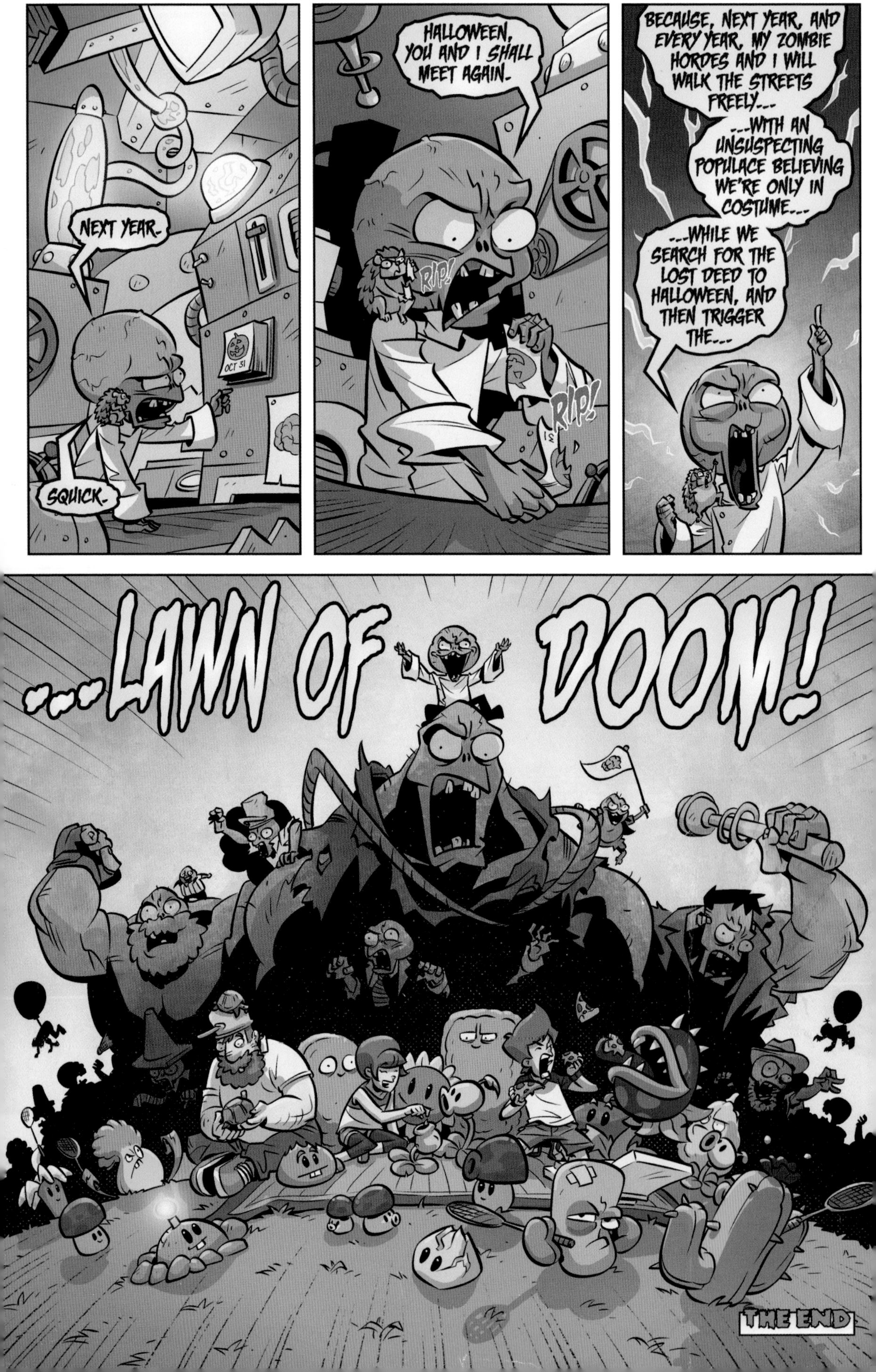
NEXT YEAR.
SQUICK.
HALLOWEEN, YOU AND I SHALL MEET AGAIN.
RIP!
RIP!
BECAUSE, NEXT YEAR, AND EVERY YEAR, MY ZOMBIE HORDES AND I WILL WALK THE STREETS FREELY...
...WITH AN UNSUSPECTING POPULACE BELIEVING WE'RE ONLY IN COSTUME...
...WHILE WE SEARCH FOR THE LOST DEED TO HALLOWEEN, AND THEN TRIGGER THE...
...LAWN OF DOOM!
THE END